# RED SHIFT
# RATES
# RAVE REVIEWS

"Alan Garner is one of the most challenging nov-
elists writing today and *Red Shift* is a work of poetic
imagination that will keep any adult mind at full
stretch. It is a contemporary disenchanted Romeo
and Juliet story."

—*Daily Mail*

"He squeezes language into depth charges which
will detonate emotions at a level where words cannot reach . . . The past, when he compresses it into
the shapes of myth and spell, is energy, electricity,
more life for those who can top it. To unlock the
folk-memory of the soil you stand on is to arm
yourself with power and passion from the genera-
tions who have lived there before you."

—*The Listener*

"Its impact leaves one with no doubt that Alan
Garner is a daring, exciting, ambitious writer."

—*Birmingham Post*

Also by Alan Garner
*Published by Ballantine Books:*

ELIDOR

THE OWL SERVICE

THE WEIRDSTONE OF BRISINGAMEN

THE MOON OF GOMRATH

# RED SHIFT

*Alan Garner*

A Del Rey Book

BALLANTINE BOOKS • NEW YORK

For Billy

Published in Great Britain by William Collins Sons & Co.
Ltd. 1973

A Del Rey Book
Published by Ballantine Books

Copyright © 1973 Alan Garner

Library of Congress Catalog Card Number: 73-584

ISBN 0-345-30071-8

This edition published by arrangement with
William Collins Sons & Co. Ltd.

Manufactured in the United States of America

First Ballantine Books Edition: November 1981

Cover art by Laurence Schwinger

"Shall I tell you?"

"What?"

"Shall I?"

"Tell me what?" said Jan.

"What do you want to know?"

Jan picked up a fistful of earth and trickled it down the neck of his shirt.

"Hey!"

"Stop fooling, then."

Tom shook his trouser legs. "That's rotten. I'm all gritty."

Jan hung her arms over the motorway fence. Cars went by like brush marks. "Where are they going? They look so serious."

"Well," said Tom. "Let's work it out. That one there is travelling south at, say, one hundred and twenty kilometers per hour, on a continental shelf drifting east at about five centimetres per year—"

"I might've guessed—!"

"—on a planet rotating at about nine hundred and ninety kilometres per hour at this degree of latitude, at a mean orbital velocity of thirty kilometres per second—"

"Really?"

"—in a solar system travelling at a mean galactic velocity of twenty-five kilometres per second, in a galaxy that probably has a random motion—"

"Knickers."

"—random knickers of about one hundred kilometres per second in a universe that appears to be expanding at about one hundred and sixteen kilometres per second per megaparsec."

1

Jan scooped up more earth.

"The short answer's Birmingham," he said, and ducked.

Jan looked across the flooded sand quarry behind them towards the Rudheath caravan site among the birch trees. "Come on." The earth was still in her hand.

"Where?"

"What were you going to tell me?"

"Oh, that." He took his shoe off and turned it upside down. "It really is grotty being gritty. I was going to tell you when I first saw you."

"When was it?"

"When you came back from Germany."

"Germany?" The earth ran through her fingers. "Germany? We've known each other longer than that."

"But I didn't see you until you got out of the car: and then I—saw you."

"I wasn't away more than a fortnight."

"What was it like?"

"Anywhere."

"The people you stayed with?"

"Ordinary."

"So why go?"

"To see what it was like."

"And she found that the ground was as hard, that a yard was as long—No. She found that a metre was neater—"

"Tom—"

"Yes?"

"Lay off."

He put his head on her shoulder. "I couldn't stand it if you went now," he said. They walked from the motorway fence along a spit of sand between the lakes.

" 'Grotty' is excessively ugly," said Tom. "A corruption of 'grotesque.' It won't last."

"I love you."

"I'm not sure about the mean galactic velocity. We're with M31, M32, M33 and a couple of dozen other galaxies. They're the nearest. What did you say?"

"I love you."

"Yes." He stopped walking. "That's all we can be sure of. We are, at this moment, somewhere between the M6 going to Birmingham and M33 going nowhere. Don't leave me."

"Hush," said Jan. "It's all right."

"It's not. How did we meet? How could we? Between the M6 and M33. Think of the odds. In all space and time. I'm scared."

"Don't be."

"Scared of losing——"

"You're not——"

"I always win."

She pressed the back of her hand against his cheek.

"Tell me," he said. "I've been waiting all afternoon."

The motorway roared silently. Birds skittered the water in flight to more distant reeds, and the iron water lay again, flat light reflecting no sky. The caravans and the birches. Tom.

"Next week," said Jan. "Right?" Her knuckles were comfortless between his. "Next week. I go next week." She tried to reach the pain, but his eyes would not let her in.

"London?"

"Yes." Teeth showing through lips drawn: lines from sides of nostrils: frown and pain lines. "And my parents——"

"It's a pretty mean galaxy."

She pulled him to her. "You're just a baby."

"Yes."

"Upset."

"I'm not upset. I'm panicking. Love me."

"I do. I do love you."

"For ever."

"How——"

"Love is not love which alters when it alteration finds."

"Quote."

3

"More know Tom Fool than Tom Fool knows. And that's another." He stood back from her and bent down to skim a stone across the lake. "On one side lay the M6, and on one lay a great water, and the site was full. Seven bounces! Bet you can't do more than three!"

"Which of you am I supposed to believe?" said Jan.

"Both."

"When will you grow up?"

"We were born grown up."

"I love you: you idiots."

They went round the caravan site by the sand washer. It was a tower, with chutes that fed sand into a piled cone. There was a catwalk to the top, over the chutes. The top was a very small steel plate.

Tom ran up and climbed to the plate. He stood slowly, feeling for his balance. The sand pile was a perfect gradient, one in one. Tom spread his arms, thirty feet above the ground.

"If you drop," he called to Jan, "it doesn't half rattle your teeth. But if you jump out as far as you can, it's flying, and you hit the sand at the same angle right at the bottom, no trouble. It's the first time that grips. You have to trust."

He leapt through the air clear of everything and ploughed the sand with his heels.

"Coming?" He looked up at her.

"No thanks."

"It's not what it seems. Or aren't you good on heights?"

"I don't like being gritty."

They crossed the road to the houses where Jan lived.

"That was fairly stupid," said Tom.

"I was impressed."

"Not the jump. That was stupid, but the other was worse."

"It's happened before."

"And it'll happen again."

"I know."

"Stupid and infantile."

4

They were clear of the birch wood, by open fields. Television screens in the caravans flickered among the white bark.

"Corpse candles," said Tom.

"Snob. They look cosy."

"They are. Togetherness!"

"Don't take it out on them. I'd rather not live in London; but I do want to nurse. It's as simple as that."

"I wasn't stopping you."

"You weren't?"

"We'll adapt," he said. "You'll get a fair bit of time off, even in training, and you can come home. It's quick from London. I'm used to you every day, that's all, knowing I'll see you— Oh my God."

Two men were putting up a *For Sale* notice in Jan's garden.

"I was trying to tell you," she said.

"No one does this to me."

"No one's doing anything to anybody."

"What's that, then?"

"I was trying to tell you. Mum and Dad have been given a unit in Portsmouth. We're all moving. We've never stayed long anywhere."

"I reckon it's a pretty mean galaxy."

He took a key out of his pocket and unlocked the door. They went inside the house. There was a red light on the telephone-answering machine. Jan pulled a face.

"What's the matter?" said Tom.

"Mum has a patient who rings every day. It's rubbish."

"Not to him at the other end."

"Precisely."

"How can they stay sane, doing that work?"

"They never let themselves be involved. It's in the training."

"But they're always on call, especially with that thing."

"What, the Tam? There are some patients who'd rather talk to a phone than to Mum or Dad."

"Get away."

5

"They would. They feel safer. A tape recorder doesn't want things from them."

"A cassette confessor."

"If you like."

"An automatic answering divine. God in the machine."

"Don't be daft," said Jan. "It's only something that helps two people help a lot of others. It means they're never out of touch."

"Or never in."

"They're busy." She switched the tape on and spoke into the telephone. "This is Jan. I'm going to the caravan for tea, then Tom's coming back to work."

"Do you ever meet?" said Tom.

"I didn't ask for that."

"Sorry."

"OK. But it wasn't funny."

"No."

They sat by the fire; landscapes were in the coals.

"Are you sulking?" said Jan.

"Thinking."

"What?"

"Plans."

"Secret?"

"No." Tom fingered the stonework of the hearth. "I'll miss this nonentity box."

"I shan't," said Jan. "All our houses are bland, wherever we go. Dad had to buy and sell quickly."

"It's better than a caravan. It gives you room. Every way. Plenty of space for ducks on these walls."

"You're a snob."

"Inverted," said Tom. "I made my father a regimental gnome when I was ten: spent weeks of Free Expression on it at school."

"What happened?"

"It melted in the rain. But he was chuffed at the time."

"Will you be able to work in the caravan?"

"Not as well as I can here, but I'll manage. Anybody can pass exams."

"You're spooking me. You're too quiet."

6

He put his head on the stone. "I'm not very quiet inside. Come on. Let's go. Forget the house. It's only a waiting room now."

The men had stopped their hammering.

It was dark in the birch wood among the caravans. People moved along the cinder roads, carrying buckets. On every screen, the same wrestler bounced off the same ropes into the same forearm smash.

"It was recorded last week," said Tom.

They reached Tom's caravan. His father's topiary, privet grown in ammunition boxes, stood along the front, the rope handles stiff with white gloss paint.

Tom and Jan kicked off their shoes as they entered. Now the crowd could be heard, and the bell for the fifth round.

"Leave your boots in the vestibule," Tom's mother called from the lounge.

"Have done. What's the score?"

"One each. A folding press and a back-breaker submission."

"I've worked it out," he said to Jan. "We'll be all right. Tell you later."

They went into the kitchen. His father had laid the table, and was tossing lettuce in a dressing.

"Smells good," said Jan. "What is it?"

"Wine vinegar and dill."

"I always drop the salad on the floor," said Jan.

"The secret's in the bowl. Use one a lot bigger than you think you need: give yourself plenty of room."

"I estimate that salad has proportionately more space allocated to it than I have," said Tom. "Permission to be a lettuce, sir, please."

"Permission refused," said his father.

"Carry on, sergeant-major," said Tom, and went to lie on his bunk.

Through the partition wall he could hear the television commentary, and a few feet away Jan and his father were discussing salad. "Boston Crab and Cold Lobster do not mix," he wrote in his Physics notebook.

He took from behind the pillow a pair of army headphones which he had padded with rubber. He clipped the can over his head, and was private again. Jan and his father made the rest of the salad, and he watched them as if they were in an aquarium. On the caravan wall, framed, were his great-grandfather's war medals, and beneath them his grandfather's. His father's uniform hung, ready for duty, the one ribbon, for Long Service and Good Conduct, clean, new crimson and silver.

He felt his mother pass by from the lounge and saw her go into the kitchen to fry herself some bacon. The smell came through the silence. Then Jan was with him, smiling, reaching out her hand. He took off the cans and entered the aquarium.

"Single-leg Boston in the last round," his mother said. "After two public Warnings."

"So long as the damage is done, warnings don't count," said his father.

The lobster lay dismembered in a bed of lettuce. "Seems a pity to spoil it," said Jan.

"Ask the lobster," said Tom, and filled his plate.

Tom's mother cut off the bacon rind and ate it. "The nights are drawing in."

"As Thomas à Becket said to the actress."

Jan sputtered.

"You what?" said his mother.

"How's the dressing?" said Tom's father.

"Delicious," said Jan.

"Let's see how you do with the wine, then. I've a poser for you this week."

"You wily warrant-officer," said Tom. "You've decanted it."

"All's fair in love and war. Couldn't have you seeing the bottle, could we?"

He poured the green-white wine for Tom and Jan. Tom's mother put the kettle on the stove to make herself some tea. "Never stake money on a bet with this man," said Tom. "He waited till we'd had the dressing."

"That's your manky palate, lad. The dressing and the wine have to balance. There's the art."

"It's a Moselle," said Jan. "Very fresh. Last year's, I think."

Tom's father stared. "How did you know? Come off it: that wasn't a guess."

"I was *au pair* for a grower at Easter," said Jan. "Moselle."

"Ay, you can't win 'em all. Lovely wine, though, isn't it? The only good thing to come out of Germany."

"What about the iron crosses hanging with the medals?" said Tom.

"They weren't from walking-wounded, I can tell you."

"Swapped for a packet of fags?"

"Hand to hand. Them or us. That's our mob."

Tom turned to Jan. "We don't count that. You'd been there—What's the matter?"

Jan stumbled from the chair, her handkerchief at her mouth.

"Not the bog!" Tom shouted after her. "I've not emptied it this week!"

Jan threw the door open and was sick into the bracken.

"So much for your fancy teas," said Tom's mother. "Well, it had to show sooner or later."

Jan came back into the caravan. "Sorry," she said. "Do you think I could have a glass of water?"

"Sit down," said Tom's father. "I'll get it."

"Thanks."

"Here you are."

"Do you mind if I take it outside? I want to rinse my mouth."

"Not before time," said Tom's mother.

Tom followed Jan out to the steps and put his anorak round her. She was shivering. He went down the steps and turned the leaf mould over with a spade.

"One of the benefits of the rural life," he said. He came back to her. "What's up, apart from the lobster?"

"Sea food gets me sometimes."

"Indeed."

She shrugged. "I'm fine now."

"At least you're human. I thought you weren't bothered by next week."

"I'm bothered, all right."

Tom's father was finishing the meal, but his mother had taken her tea through to the lounge.

"Better?"

"Thanks. It sometimes gets me."

"You should've said. Can I make you anything?"

"A piece of bread will do fine."

"Moselle?"

"I'd rather not. Sorry. It was a lovely meal."

"Moselle's good for an upset stomach."

"No thanks."

"Your colour's back."

"I'll finish your wine," said Tom.

"Show it a little respect," said his father. "It's not lemonade."

"To the glorious dead German grape." Tom raised his glass.

"Cider's the worst," said his father.

Tom and Jan cleared the table.

"You feel it in your bones next day. Soon as you drink anything—tea, milk, water—you're as stoned as when you began. Wicked."

"Courting time," said Jan. "All ancients into the lounge."

"Ay, well," said Tom's father. "Think on." He closed the kitchen door after him.

Tom poured the last of the wine. He hid his face in Jan's hair. She stepped away.

"What's wrong now?"

"I don't like the smell of drink," she said.

"Have some, then you won't notice." She shook her head. "Your loss." He emptied the glass.

"Let's wash up." Jan pulled on a pair of rubber gloves and ran hot water into the sink. Tom picked up a towel.

"There's something bothering your father. He wasn't himself."

"Wasn't he? Look, I've worked it all out. On your

10

pay, and what I can scrounge, we should just about be able to meet, say, every month. Crewe."

"Why not come here? It's not that much further."

"Crewe's quicker, and we shan't waste time we could spend together. No privacy here. We couldn't talk. If you make it Saturdays, the shops'll be open, and it'll be warm."

"I've never felt romantic in Crewe."

"You will. It'll be the most fabulous town on earth."

Jan gave him a plate to dry. "Fantastic," she said. The kitchen door opened, and Tom's father appeared.

"Er."

"Yes?" said Tom.

"My glasses."

"By the telly?" said Jan.

"Oh. Feeling better?"

"Right as rain."

"Good." He went out.

"There's definitely something wrong," said Jan. "He's embarrassed. And listen: they're arguing."

"When aren't they? I'm sorry I panicked at the motorway. We'll be OK.—I wonder why rain is always right."

"Didn't you see him?"

"No. We'll be OK in Crewe. You can get a cheap day-return."

"Listen!" She held his shoulders. Warmth seeped through and bubbles rainbowed his shirt.

"You're wonderful," he said. "Your eyes are like poached eggs."

"Tom, listen. Something's wrong— What did you say?"

"Poached eggs. Round and meaningful. I cherish them."

Jan laughed and wept onto his chest, hugging him. "You lovely bloody idiot. What am I going to do?"

"Don't swear. It demeans you. Poached isn't the same as hard-boiled. I love your face."

"I love you."

The kitchen door opened. Tom's mother stood with uninterrupted vision. His father was with her.

"Is there no privacy in this camp coffin?" said Tom.

"Your mother and I would like a word with you. Both of you."

"Why?"

"In the lounge."

"It's Sunday, sergeant-major. We have the kitchen, and you have the lounge."

Jan led the way to the other end of the caravan. Tom's father turned off the volume control on the television.

"It must be serious," said Tom.

"Shut up," said Jan.

"Sit down: will you—please? On the divan."

They sat. Tom's father went to the window and peered out, half facing the room, his hands behind his back. "Stand easy," said Tom. His mother lodged one buttock on the arm of a chair, swinging her foot.

"I want to ask—"

"What?"

"I want to ask you and Jan—"

"What?"

"It's written all over you," said his mother.

"Your mother and I—would like to know whether you've anything to tell us."

"What's your problem?" Tom reached out his hand for Jan. She took it.

"We think—"

"Both of you?"

"Don't," said Jan.

"I'm trying to be useful," said Tom.

"Like hell."

"Watch that tongue of yours!" said Tom's mother.

"She'd look pretty silly if she did."

"Stop arsing around," Jan whispered.

"I heard that!"

"Let's try again," his father said.

Tom opened his mouth, but Jan kicked him.

"Your mother and I. We wondered if you'd had

12

any occasion to do anything to make us ashamed of you.

Tom stared at the muted commercials on the television screen. I'm wearing my cans. Please, I'm wearing my cans.

"Well?"

"Would you care to rephrase the question in English?"

"You heard me." His father was shouting: he could see him.

"Yes. We have."

"What did I tell you?" said his mother.

"What did she?"

A silent boy poured cornflakes silently into a bowl of light, and smiled.

"When?" said Tom's father. "When did you?"

"When did we what? Look, sergeant-major, I've a pile of work to get through tonight——"

"When did you have occasion——"

"——to make you ashamed of us? Last Saturday."

"What?"

"We went by bus to Sandbach without paying."

"What's eating them?" Jan said to Tom in Russian.

Tom stood up. He was shaking. There were no cans. He spoke clearly.

"My parents are trying to articulate—or, more accurately, my prurient mother is forcing my weak father to discover on her behalf, where, when, and preferably how, we, that is, you and I, have expressed ourselves through sexual intercourse, one with the other. Am I not right? Daddy?"

His father grasped the side seams of his trousers, rocked as if he would fall.

"What did I tell you?"

"Yes, what did she tell you?"

His father steadied himself. "We've had complaints."

"Complaints?"

"Reports."

"Reports?"

"Yes."

"From whom?"

"Neighbors."

"May we know their names?"

"Never mind who," said his mother. "We've heard and seen. You two: always walked wrapped round each other: kissing and that."

"Kissing and what?"

"And—that."

Cans.

"And the time you spend in that house alone. Do her parents know?"

"Of course," said Jan.

"Then they ought to know better."

"Than what?"

"Than to let you get up to things in their own home."

"It's the only," screamed Tom, "place I could ever work without your clattering: drivelling: the weather! The only—keep books clean! Jan first ever," his eyes were shut, "see anything. anything in me. worth. anything." He rammed the backs of his fists into his face, dragging his eyes open.

"I do not propose to discuss our relationship, or matters appertaining to it, beyond that statement. I will be private, sergeant-major. I will be private sergeant-major—" He meant to laugh, but the trembling reached his throat. He stood, his father's size, broken.

"You great wet Nelly," said his father. "You're as much use as a chocolate teapot."

"Is Tom right?" said Jan. "Is that why you've done it?"

"What can't speak can't lie," said his mother. "I can read that one like a book."

"You cow. You think we've been having it off together, don't you?"

"I've told you to watch your filthy tongue, young woman."

"You're afraid," said Jan. "Afraid we're doing what you did when you had the chance. And what if we

14

have? Who are you to preach? I bet you've flattened some grass in your time."

Tom ran from the room.

"That's no way to speak."

"Sorry, sergeant-major. Will you excuse me? I must see how Tom is after your achievement."

"I knew what you were the moment I set eyes on you," said Tom's mother. "I felt a shiver right down my spine. And our boy. See what you've done to him. Standing there, crying his heart out. Couldn't look his own mother in the face. Couldn't deny it: not even his fancy words could get round that one."

"Oh, piss off, you," said Jan, and slammed the door.

She found Tom leaning across the sink, his head on his arms against the window glass. The sobbing came from his stomach, shook the caravan. His sleeve had dragged a clean line through the condensation, and his giant shadow was on the wood outside, like a hole in space among the white birches.

Jan put her arms round him, stroked, kissed, "It's all right, it's all right," but the spasms of his weeping shook her, would not be subdued.

"How dare they—?"

"Hush, love, it's all right." Both taps of the sink had been twisted out of shape, but Tom's hands were not marked. "It's all right; I'm here."

"How dare they try—how dare they—how dare they try to—?" He pressed his open palms against the window gently, relentlessly, so that it broke without shattering, and the glass collapsed only when he moved his hands.

"Tom!"

He held the fragments like crushed ice. Shallow, pale lines crazed his skin. He felt nothing.

The hard, smooth terror was in him. He saw the birches carved, bent to shapes that were not trees but men, animals, and the hardness and the terror were blue and silver on the edge of vision. He opened his cloak, and Logan saw him strike at the guard with

15

something smooth held between his hands. The guard fell, and Macey jumped from the road to the ditch.

"Follow the kid!" shouted Logan. "Move!"

They drove for the wood. Logan snatched the rein of a pack mule. The air thrummed and hissed arrows. The mule's baggage was a shield, but Logan stumbled over men on the open ground.

Macey was behind a birch, wiping his hands on rags, wrapping, thrusting the rags under his cloak.

"Come on, kid!"

"No," said Macey. "Stop. And the others."

"Move!"

"No."

The guards were still on the road. They had not followed.

Macey went to the edge of the trees. "This," he called across the ditch, "for all men, in the name of the keeper of the place."

"Don't push it," said Logan.

"They won't touch sanctuary," said Buzzard.

Logan looked about him at the worked trees. "Where are we?"

"Rudheath."

"It's a Cats' sanctuary," said Face.

"And Cats is allies," said Magoo.

"The country's federation ground hereabouts," said Buzzard.

"Federation ballocks," said Magoo. "Cats is Cats."

"I don't trust nobody past Crewe," said Logan. "Get further into the wood."

They retreated until the guards and the road were lost.

"How good's this sanctuary?" said Logan.

"Depends how the Cats rate it," said Face, "and what they figure the army'll pay to get us back."

"The road must've clipped the sanctuary," said Buzzard. "Reckon the army won't be too popular."

"We need hardware," said Magoo. "Ain't nothing on the mule."

"Go see what you can find on the dead guys," said Logan. "There may be a knife or something."

16

"Lotta use that'll be," said Face.

"It's a start."

"We was marching degraded, remember?" said Magoo. "Hey, what was that Macey pulled on the guard?"

"Not!" said Macey. He sat by a tree. Sweat from his hand had soaked the rags. The hardness wrapped in tatters hung at his shoulder, beneath his cloak. The weight of it was heavy for the first time, heavier than anything ever.

"Aw, come on, goofball."

"He said no." Logan watched the men.

"What'll we do?" said Face.

"We'll soldier," said Logan. "We're the Ninth."

"There ain't no Ninth," said Face. "Why are you carrying on like we wasn't busted?"

"I don't give a toss what some minging stonemason does because he thinks he can run an army. Let him build his goddam wall, and the rest of the crap, but we're still the Ninth, not brickies. Right?"

They looked at each other, and at the sanctuary.

"Yeh."

"Anybody claim rank over me?" said Logan. "Right. We're back on duty. Military discipline will apply. Face, Buzzard, check out this place. You still waiting?" he said to Magoo.

Macey was inert, wrapped in his cloak. "My mates," he said.

Logan tethered the mule. "That was pretty smart, kid. I thought you'd flipped."

Macey looked up at him. He seemed to be terrified.

"We'd all've gone if you hadn't used it," said Logan.

"You didn't see."

"I saw enough."

"You mustn't see!"

"You used the stone axe from way back."

"No. They're never used."

Logan held out his hand. "I'd sure appreciate it—"

"No! But I had to. You're my mates. Not for me. My mates."

"Yeh, we're your mates. It was OK. Quit worrying."

"Brilliant mates. All brilliant mates."

"You were right, kid. I saw nothing."

"I saw."

"Saw what?"

"Blue. Silver. And red."

"What's with this blue and silver? You ever had it before?"

"When I was a kid. Pain. But then it was— Hell, there ain't words."

"Like you flipped?"

"But I didn't go," said Macey. "Blue and silver— makes me so chickenshit I can't remember whatall next. It was changing. But when—that guy—killed him hereabouts—when I killed him—on the road— blue and silver—I freaked—but I could see him, what I did—but there was two hands—pressing at me—a long way off against my eyes—and then near—and then noplace—big as all there is. Sir, I don't think I'm too good for this unit any more."

Magoo appeared among the trees. "Nothing," he said. "And there's no guards."

"Scived back to Chester," said Logan. "I'd like to see their report!"

"I don't figure they'll be making none. Sir."

"Why?"

Magoo smiled, and went back towards the road. Logan followed.

"They've taken the bodies."

"Reckon?" said Magoo.

They stood by the road. It was empty and straight, the cleared ground on either side hid no one.

On the road, blood still moved. It lay in patches for a hundred metres. The guards had tried to run. There was nothing left.

"Did you hear?" said Logan.

"No."

"What, then?"

"We're past Crewe. Like you said."

"Back on sanctuary. Quick."

Buzzard was hurrying to meet them as they crossed

the ditch. "Sir!" Face and me: we've found the shrine. It don't look healthy."

"Show," said Logan.

They went into the birch wood. Every tree had rags tied to it: in a clearing they came to a spring, and around it were offerings of human heads.

"What tribe?" said Logan.

"Cats."

"But the trees are Cat totems."

"Look at the spring, sir."

The water emerged from above a line of clay, but recently, so recently that the earth had not crumbled, the bank had been cut back to hold a stone through which the water ran, and the front of the stone was carved as a snake, open-mouthed.

"How do you read?" said Logan.

"Not more than a week old," said Magoo, turning a head between his hands. "The stone's new."

"Reconsecration," said Buzzard. "By the Mothers. They're moving south."

"Stand to. All arms," said Logan. "At the double here."

"Yessir."

They brought Macey and the pack mule.

"Alternative analysis?" said Logan.

"None, sir," said Buzzard. "This is a Mothers snake, and those heads are Cats."

"Will they be near?"

"Unlikely," said Face. "They're scared of their own sanctuaries. They'll come if they've any Cats to sacrifice."

"You and Magoo stand sentry," said Logan, "but listen. All of you get this, and get it good. The guards have been taken out, maybe not by Cats. The Mothers have come south. They'll raid the Cats wherever they find them, and both sides will whip our ass if we let them. Solutions."

"The usual," said Face. "Divide and rule. Hit the infrastructure."

"Correct. All right? We retreat until we're clear of the Mothers, then we go tribal."

"What about you, sir?" said Buzzard.

"I can pass. I know enough to get by, but when things stabilize here, we'll have to settle for one dialect."

"There's only one," said Magoo, and laughed. "Who'd've thought the Ninth would end up as frigging Mothers!"

"We're still the Ninth," said Logan. "But we're fighting a different war." He pulled out the snake from the spring mouth and broke it. He left the pieces as they lay. "Bury the heads. Then move. Single file. South-east. Kill on sight."

"What with?" said Buzzard.

"Anything. We're fighting a different war. You've one chance, if you're smart, and there's one way to know you won't be double-crossed. That applies at all times."

"All mates: all we've got," said Macey. "All we need."

"What was it you pulled on the guard?" said Magoo. "I've marched with you five years and never saw. What was it?"

"No," said Macey, hugging himself.

"Aw, don't be like that. We're your mates, goofball." He tried to wrestle with him.

Logan's boot came down on Magoo's wrist. "I'll kill any man who touches Macey's gear. No questions. A military order. Acknowledge."

"Affirmative," said the Ninth.

They withdrew slowly, hiding their tracks. Buzzard led, Macey held the mule and Logan covered the rear. They swung into deep forest away from the road. It was quiet in the forest, as if sanctuary moved with them.

They halted at the lip of a steep river valley. "The Dane," said Buzzard. "It's fordable."

Face climbed a tree. "We're on course," he said when he came down. "Sanctuary bearing three-five-zero, and a mountain, bearing one-three-zero, estimated eleven clicks. But we'll need to swing south to avoid towns. They'll be full of Cats wanting protection right now, so we'd better watch out when we cross the Sandbach road. There'll be heavy traffic."

"Mountain status," said Logan.

"Isolated peak," said Buzzard. "Mow Cop. Ridge running north. Gap near Bosley, where Cats have federal permission to fortify a camp. Suggest ideal, but cold, sir."

"We'd see them coming."

"Militarily strong, good water, but severe exposure."

"Right," said Logan. "Maintain present bearing. Cross Sandbach road, then swing for Mow Cop. And I want me a Cat village before dark."

"We could reach Mow Cop in daylight, sir."

"It's not that easy."

"How big a village, sir?"

"Big enough to equip us, not too big to take."

They crossed all tracks, followed none.

"Mow Cop bearing eight-zero," said Face, "ten clicks. And I smelt smoke: wind one-seven-zero."

"Report," Logan said to Buzzard.

Buzzard went up the tree. "Domestic," he said.

"Not a raid?"

"Negative."

"Distance?"

"Estimated three clicks."

"Tether and blindfold the mule," Logan said to Macey. "Magoo, Face, go see that village. Full logistics and report back before dusk."

"Yessir."

"You all right, kid?" said Logan.

"I guess so."

"We'll be depending on you. Your mates. You won't chicken?"

"I hope not, sir."

"Kip down: Buzzard and I'll stand to."

"What do you plan?" said Buzzard.

"I don't know yet," said Logan.

"Why smash that snake? Sure, they were the Mothers, but I've never known you violate gods. Even Magoo was shook up. Hit the infrastructure, yeh, but in the Ninth we always said Logan—"

21

"In the Ninth we still say."

"Sir?"

"We still say, we still think, we still do. The Ninth functions."

"Yessir."

"Sound more convinced."

"I'd just like to report," said Buzzard, "that if we're the Ninth, we're understrength."

"I can't sleep, sir," said Macey.

"Lie quiet: rest."

"What are you figuring on?" said Buzzard.

"I don't know yet," said Logan.

Face and Magoo returned.

"Small settlement," said Face. "I've seen it before. Called Barthomley. Cats. One roundhut: two, three others: estimated twenty men plus families. Situated on low mound, stream to the north at foot called Wulvarn. One gate, shut, guarded: simple ditch and stockade. Four sentries in all. Ditch filled with green thorns."

"Attitude," said Logan.

"Defensive only."

"Trained?"

"Negative."

"We can take 'em," said Magoo. "If we throw the pack tent across the thorns, the stockade's only three metres."

"Noted," said Logan.

They led the mule to within half a kilometre of the settlement, then Logan ordered a halt. It was night and a clear moon.

"Buzzard, I want you to go in there and bring back one sword."

"You kidding?" said Buzzard.

"Get."

Buzzard hesitated.

"Make with that sword," said Logan.

He was away an hour. The blade was long.

"You can use this?" Logan said to Macey.

"Guess I can."

"Sir," said Buzzard, "Them Cats is easy. They're

farmers. Who needs Macey? Shout 'Mothers' over the fence and they'll die."

"Good," said Logan. "Now we're going to take out this village with tribal weapons, OK? I figure for the Ninth to survive it must disappear. They won't put this one down to us. We maximise harassment and interdiction. OK?"

Magoo grinned. "Outta sight!"

"Here's how it is," said Logan. "Macey flips. We go in across the tent and pull it after us. When we hit their perimeter, Macey should kill four, five just like that. We grab assets, then eliminate. Result, a raid put down to the Mothers, and we have the gear to go tribal. As the Ninth, there will be no abort; but if we louse it up, survivors cut ass out on their own. Questions?"

"We hit this village," said Buzzard.

"Correct."

"And they don't know it's us."

"They know," said Logan. "But that's all."

"Children. Women."

"Wise up," said Magoo.

"I told you," said Logan, "we're fighting a different war."

"I can't do that cold," said Buzzard.

"You won't be cold," said Magoo.

Macey could hardly walk. Logan and Face took an elbow each to steady his trembling. Logan held the sword.

"You'll be OK soon, kid. This is the worst. You're with your mates."

The village was only an enclosure on a long, low mound above a stream.

"How's that water?" said Logan.

"Clear," said Face. "Bog the other side. I suggest we hit near the gate."

"Agreed," said Logan, and settled Macey on the ground, with the sword hilt between his hands, like a child with an unknown toy.

"Why don't we try it easy, first?" said Buzzard. "Like ask them to let us in."

"You crazy?" said Magoo.

"No, but Macey is. And when he turns on, he ain't exactly quiet, neither."

"Right," said Magoo.

"Surprise is all we got," said Face.

"They don't know that," said Logan.

"I've been in," said Buzzard. "They don't want trouble, but they're sure scared."

"And they don't come more dangerous than then," said Face.

"Go talk to them," Logan ordered Buzzard. "Say we're a patrol and we've a wounded man. That'll cover Macey. But don't let them open the gate. Say there's Mothers about."

"You may not be fooling," said Magoo.

"Go with him," said Logan, "and as soon as Macey's across them thorns, you and Buzzard drag the tent over. It's deployed?"

"Yessir."

They went through the forest towards the camp.

Face twisted a harness round Macey's shoulders, holding him upright against a tree. Logan worked the leather down to Macey's elbows. "Keep close behind that trunk," he said.

"You bet," said Face.

"What you want for light, kid?" said Logan. "There's a moon."

"No!" Macey struggled.

"Steady," said Logan. "Not yet. We gotta have light. Stars OK?"

"Yes."

"Well, look there, kid. If that ain't old Orion up in the sky. Can you see his belt? Three bright stars. Which of those pretty little stars are you going to be?"

Voices, not loud, came from the camp.

"Take no notice," said Logan. "You choose yourself a pretty twinkling star on Orion's belt. OK?"

"OK."

"Which one?"

"—Mintaka."

24

"Mintaka. Right. Now you keep watching old Mintaka, and see that son of a bitch don't run away."

Logan took out of his cloak a small wheel from a horse trapping. It was held between two prongs like the rowel of a spur.

"You keep looking at Mintaka: and catch hold of that sword now."

Face gripped the harness and pressed his head and body against the opposite side of the tree. Logan spun the wheel, flickering starlight. He stroked the rim with an accustomed measure, evenly turning the spokes, their invisible shadows glimmering Macey's eye.

The voices at the camp argued, but there was no alarm.

"Go, Macey. Mintaka, baby. Go, kid."

Macey shook:

"Go, baby, go." The hand caressed, the wheel spun. "Go, baby."

Face frowned at Logan, puzzled.

"Mintaka. Mintaka. Stay loose, kid. You gotta go."

Macey's eye was open. Logan stopped speaking. The sound between them was the thin ring of the wheel.

"Mintaka, baby."

Macey sagged in his harness, his head drooped.

"I can't make it." He was crying. "I can't flip."

"Get down with the others," Logan said to Face. "Be ready."

"But he's—"

"Get down." Logan twistd the harness into his own hand, and put the wheel away. "Get down."

"Sir, he ain't safe for one man."

"I'm ordering you."

Face backed off until he was clear.

"What is it, kid? You want to try the moon?"

"The moon's axe edge," sobbed Macey.

"Yeh! Those are your words, kid! You're remembering!"

"I am the one the moon's axe spares—"

"Great! Great!"

25

"No, sir. I can't flip with no axe, no smoothe hard axe. Not now."

"But it's safe, kid. Stay loose. You've got the axe from way back."

"It don't talk to me no more."

Logan bit on the harness, his look upon the glow of the camp. Macey's head was young.

"You ain't gonna flip?"

"Not really, sir."

"OK," said Logan. "No Ninth. No brilliant mates. Finish."

"I ain't brilliant now, sir. Not any more."

"You ain't. You ain't brilliant, kid. You're blue and silver."

Macey screamed.

"Blue and silver, blue, silver."

Macey screamed again as each word tore him. Logan felt the strength and agony in the harness.

"Go, baby, bluesilver blue silver!"

He watched the sword, ready for spasm.

"Bluesilver, bluesilver, bluesilver, red, baby!"

Macey was rigid against the tree. His arms brought the sword up in front of him, pointing at the camp.

"Yeh, that's your bluesilver. Go take it. Take them bluesilver bastards in there!" Logan slackened the harness, whistled the warning to Magoo, Face and Buzzard. "Go take them bluesilvers!"

"Let there be no strife," shouted Macey, "for we are brothers! The distance is gone between us!"

"Chickenshit! Where's the big words! Come on! You've flipped! The big words, so's you can go!"

"The strong bull of earth!" sang Macey. "The white bull bellows!"

"That's it, kid!"

"I am above you!

"I am a man!

"I am the man of all gifts and all giving!

"Prepare my way for me!"

"You're there!" Logan threw off the harness. But Macey jerked with a force that Logan had never felt

26

in him. The sword still pointed, but the body was too rigid to move.

"The distance is gone between us!

"Silver cloud lost!

"Blue sky away!

"Stars turn!"

Logan held on. The strength in Macey he had never known, and the words were not his.

"The wind blows—through sharp—thorns, for we are brothers, through the sharp hawthorn Tom's a cold angler in the lake of darkness, blow the winds, blow, blew, blow, silver go! Go!"

Macey broke from the tree, straight for the camp. Logan staggered after him. Magoo, Face, Buzzard fell aside and Macey ran by, across the thorn spikes, and vaulted the stockade.

"He's flipped like all get out! He's going wide open! He ain't selective!"

They pulled the tent over the ditch. Four guards had attacked Macey and lay dead. He was in the roundhut, killing startled men as they moved from sleep.

"How many?" said Logan.

"Nineteen," said Buzzard.

"Escapes?"

"Negative. We zapped them good."

"Where's Macey?"

"Usual."

"Stopped?"

"Yep. Turned right off. Crashed out. I left him spewing by the hut. He'll sleep now."

"Right," said Logan. "Magoo, you go round up what's left. Check them out, Face."

"Yessir."

Logan went to Macey, who was curled around his sword, blank-eyed, face clawed white with tears.

"Boy," said Logan. "Was that some. He ain't never gone like that before."

The women and children were being gathered into the open space before the hut.

"I don't read you here, sir," said Buzzard.

"Grow up, soldier. You've seen this before."

"That was punitive."

"And I keep telling you this is a different war, and we follow it through."

"You call this following through?"

"You tell me," said Logan, "for once. Aw, go find some hardware, if you don't like it."

"I'll do just that," said Buzzard.

There was no reaction from the people, no pleading or sounds, as they died.

Buzzard collected weapons while the killing began. "You following through, soldier?" said Logan. "You going to wear that cloak you picked up? Who made it? If you won't have those people die, they don't exist, so how come you wear a cloak that no one made? It's cold on Mow Cop, soldier, and wind blows right through cloaks that ain't real."

Buzzard flung everything to the ground and ran towards the open space: but the others had finished for him.

"Decapitate," said Logan. "Then find yourselves clothing and equipmet."

"What the hell you at?" shouted Buzzard. "Ain't this enough?"

"Tribal raid, soldier. Decapitate. They're all right. They're dead."

"Go stuff yourself," said Buzzard. "You ain't real any more, Logan: you ain't the Ninth. You're screwed."

Logan struck him under the ribs with a spear. Buzzard looked at Logan and at the spear they both held. "You Mother," said Buzzard.

"Can we afford that, sir?" said Face.

Logan drew out the spear.

"He was the best scout we ever had, that's all," said Face. "We ain't overstrength."

"You arguing?"

"No, sir."

"Decapitate, search and equip," said Logan. "I'll stand to."

28

"Come on, Face," said Magoo. "This must look for real. I'll show you."

Logan brought the pack mule in and began to load it. "Would Mothers take rye?" he called to Face.

"Yessir. They can't grow enough."

"We need it for winter," said Magoo, "and a crop. We need to keep the heads, too."

"We stay till dawn," said Logan, "then bury army gear. And Buzzard."

"Better load him, sir," said Face, "while he'll drape."

"Liquid refreshments are now being served." Magoo was braced in the opening of a hut, a grey jar in each hand. "Those Cats, they sure make beer."

Logan and Face took the jars and drank. "Man," said Face, "I needed that."

"Go see what else."

Face went into the hut. "I thought we got all," he said.

"Glad we didn't," said Magoo. "Is she one hot trot!"

"What is it?" said Logan.

"I hold the army record," said Magoo.

"We missed a girl, sir," said Face.

"Kill her."

"Not this," said Magoo. "Not yet. Rest and Recreation, sir."

"No."

"She won't be trouble. And if we're setting up on that mountain, we need a woman."

"No."

"I can't cook, sir."

"She's yours tonight," said Logan, "but that's it."

"You next, sir?"

"No."

"OK." Magoo went back into the hut.

"We ought to have a woman, sir," said Face. "Even if we're temporary up there."

"Risk," said Logan.

"Not if we hamstring her. And we can't spare anyone for fatigues, even Macey."

29

"Point noted," said Logan, drinking.

Magoo reappeared. "Face?"

"Goddam animals," said Logan.

"Have a drink," said Magoo. "We're all you've got."

"Yeh."

"Can you go tribal, sir?"

"A soldier can do anything."

"Uh-huh?"

"And still stay the Ninth."

"The Ninth bit don't bother me. It's if you can't stake out heads, or fight dirty: you won't be tribal, you won't be no Mother, and you won't be no man."

"We speak tribal as soon as we leave this stockade," said Logan.

"But you gotta think tribal," said Magoo. "Like us. You gotta feel it. That's why Buzzard's dead. You break him when he enlists, so he'll be well motivated, and then you expect him to drop it and be himself. He couldn't: He made you kill him. You're harder than Buzzard, but right now I think you should be a goddam animal."

Logan drank.

Face came out of the hut. "Feel free," he said.

"After you, sir," said Magoo.

"To hell with them," said Logan, and went into the hut.

"What do you reckon?" said Face.

"I'll tell you when he comes out," said Magoo. "If he don't give—I've seen Romans break. If he don't do it to her he's only got himself, and he don't dare look right now."

"You like Logan?"

"He's shit gone wrong. I like surviving."

"Buzzard?"

"Playing Roman. It gets you, if you let it: then you ain't nothing. Congratulations, sir."

Logan had come out.

"Yeh."

"Have a beer."

"No. The games are over. Stand to till dawn."

30

Logan picked Macey up. The sword hung on his palm. Face pulled it away.

"Here, kid," said Logan. He pushed Macey through the door opening. "Go do yourself some good."

"You know, sir?" said Magoo. "That chick was half stoned when I found her. That's why she was missed the first time."

"Search for others," said Logan. "We can't afford mistakes."

"There won't be any more," said Face. "I know these Cats."

Macey shivered in the hut. His clothes were drying on him and stiffening. His skin flaked, encrusted. He blinked in the dark hut. A girl, about fifteen years old, lay like a doll on the floor. The lamp was reflected in her eyes. There had been paint on her brow, but it was smudged to shapelessness. Macey slumped on his hands and knees. The stink of him was in his own nostrils. He touched the paint on her forehead. "Don't," he said, "be afraid," and she reached out her hand, "of me." The hand touched the hard weight slung by his shoulder, and her eyes moved to him. He fell beside her, his fingers reached gently for the lobe of her ear and held it. She smoothed his clogged hair.

Jan held Tom's wrists. He let her. She turned on the crooked tap, shook his hands free of the glass and pushed them into the water. There were no deep cuts, and she directed the jet to sluice fragments away from the skin.

"Bloody Norah!"

Tom's father had come into the kitchen.

"Let your hands dry, don't rub them," said Jan. Tom did so, his body quiet, his face red and swollen.

"Has he hurt himself?"

"He's done no hurting," said Jan.

She dabbed his hands with paper tissue. They seemed to be free of glass. His father went to the taps and the window.

"It wasn't my idea," he said.

"So much was obvious," said Jan.

"He did this."

"Yes."

"That wasn't the idea."

"It was the result."

"Bloody Norah."

"Bloody Tom," said Jan.

"What's it come to?"

"He ran out of words."

"Him? He's a walking dictionary. I don't understand him half the time. The one thing he can do is express himself."

"He's still here," said Tom. "He hasn't died, or anything convenient like that."

"I never really thought you two were—you know."

"Permission to dismiss, please, sergeant-major."

"But it wouldn't have been right to have left it to your mother."

"Left right left right left right left left—"

"She's my wife."

Tom laughed quietly.

"It matters."

"Does it?" said Tom.

"Yes, mush: it does."

Tom lifted his head. "I usually do see things too late. My father is honest," he said to Jan. "I've never known him not." He drank some water from the tap. "The powers of recovery of the human organism are remarkable. If you're admitting error to me, you must, logically, have dissociated yourself from the accusation at source while I was being constructive with the window. You told my mother that she was wrong."

"I—did—say—"

"Something."

"Yes."

"So it's my turn to help you."

"Not me: your mother."

"You differentiate?"

"It was the swearing—"

"It didn't wreck the kitchen," said Jan.

"But it wasn't nice: from a girl. And we've always given you a considerable degree of latitude."

32

"About fifty-three degrees fourteen minutes north," said Tom.

"Swearing's not nice."

"Inadequate vocabulary would be a better description," said Tom. He walked towards the lounge.

"Don't diminish yourself in there," said Jan.

Tom nearly smiled. His father moved with him, but Tom stopped. "No, sergeant-major. This is a solo. Go help Jan."

His father wavered. "Sex," he said.

"What about it?"

"It's a terrible thing."

Tom walked endlessly towards the lounge. His mother was hunched before the gas fire. For the first time he saw that she was old. He put his arms around her shoulders. She was light to raise: he held bones. Her face rested on his shoulder. He could not tell whether her crying was real.

"I'm sorry for that," he said. "But you were, and are, wrong." She shook, too, as he had shaken, and through it, within her, he felt his own strength, and was alert.

"I thought—that you—and she."

"There's no 'she.' The name is Jan."

"I thought you'd been—intimate."

The obscenity, but he held on. Words. Which to use now to end now?

"You thought we'd had relations."

His mother nodded.

"Only our parents," said Tom, "and that should be a joke."

"Your father and I would prefer it if you waited till you'd finished your studies before you had anything to do with girls."

"That could be ten years!" He was laughing now.

"Soon enough."

"Jan's a help: and their house."

"It's not our fault we can't do better than this. It'd be worse in Married Quarters. I've had some! She should wash her mouth out with carbolic."

"Stop before you start," said Tom. "And listen.

33

What you said to Jan tonight was not only untrue, it was humiliating."

"Humiliating!"

"Will you apologise?"

"To her? To that kind of language? If you tell me you've not been—I'll believe you." Generosity, thought Tom, is infinite. "But I'm not apologising to someone who uses foul language in my home."

"Wait there," said Tom. He lifted his hands from his mother's shoulders. The cotton dress was tacky and clung to him. The prints of his palms and fingers were clear. He went to the kitchen. Jan and his father had cleaned up the glass and were putting hardboard over the window.

"My mother's upset by your swearing: so am I. Will you take it back?"

"Go on, love," said his father. "Sticks and stones—"

"Sorry," said Jan. "I'm not ashamed of what I've done."

"I needed to know," said Tom.

"How are your hands?" said his father.

"Right as rain," said Tom. "I've remembered: it was Plautus."

"Who was?"

"First said 'right as rain.' Stay there until I've settled my mother."

He went through to the lounge.

"Jan doesn't feel very accommodating. And I can see her point."

"Then she's not welcome here," said his mother.

"Suit yourself. I'm going over to 'The Limes' with her now, neither to be intimate nor to have relations, but to work."

"Your hands are bleeding."

"I'll survive," said Tom. "Hey, turn the sound up on the telly: there's a commercial for removing biological stains."

"What we want," said Tom, "is a communications satellite." He walked with Jan through the wood. It was a clear moon. The M6 was like a river, and the

Milky Way a veil over the birch trees. "I suppose any would do. How's your astronomy?"

"Non-existent."

"You must know the basic constellations."

"They never fitted the pictures in the books. I like that kite, though."

"Where? Kite? Kite? That's not a kite, you goof, that's part of Orion. Those three stars are his belt."

"Well, I've always liked them."

"OK. We'll have Delta Orionis: over there on the right. It'll be with us all winter. We'll be together at least once every twenty-four hours."

"How?"

"What's a good time? Ten o'clock? Every night at ten o'clock we'll both try to look at that star, and be together because we know the other's watching, and thinking. At the same moment we'll be looking at the same thing."

"If it isn't cloudy," said Jan. "I love you: you're so impossible."

"It's impossible."

"It's not. It's a marvellous idea. That star and us. Like now."

"There's never 'now,' " said Tom. "Delta Orionis may not exist. It isn't even where we think it is. It's so far away, we're looking at it as it was when the Romans were here."

"That's why I don't like astronomy."

"But shall we have that star?"

"Yes."

"And ten o'clock."

He unlocked the door at "The Limes."

"Coffee?" said Jan.

"Please."

He settled down by the fire. The central heating was on, but a fan turned slowly behind the mock coals.

Tom worked. After three hours he stopped. He packed his briefcase. Jan sat on the hearth, watching him.

"About today," she said.

"I don't want to talk."

"Why not?"

"It's over."

"It's not. You can't sit there and plough through those books after what they did."

"I can."

"Doesn't it bother you?"

"It did. It doesn't. Wasted energy, and a nasty taste. Forget it."

"You ought to externalise the tension."

"Don't start that. I'm not a patient yet."

"You frighten me."

"Me too, so shut up and say good-night to our Celtic grandparent."

"Our what?"

He pointed to the stone of the hearth. There was a fossil in it.

"I've never noticed," said Jan. "It's beautiful."

"It's been there for the last six hundred million years, waiting for a fireplace to happen. So meet your ancestor and mine! The one and only! Cambrian! Inarticulate! Brachiopod!"

"Why didn't I know?"

"It can't talk: on account of being inarticulate. And if it could, it'd be Welsh."

"Will it come out?"

"No."

"All that time. Can't we work it loose?"

"Your Dad wouldn't appreciate it, if he's trying to sell this desirable residence."

"I've always wanted to hold something that matters."

"Try me," said Tom. "And in case I'm no good, will this do?"

He opened his hand, and held out a gilt brooch of two linked hearts. "Mizpah" was engraved on one, and on the other, "The Lord watch between me and thee when we are absent one from another."

"I'm the free offer that goes with it," said Tom.

"For me?"

"Mizpah's Hebrew: it means something like 'look forward well': the future shared, and good, whatever

36

happens. Soldiers used to give it to their wives and that."

"Where's this from?"

"It was my grandfather's. He was killed."

"Oh."

"I want you to have it."

Jan read the words again.

"Do you believe in God?" she said.

"I hope he believes in me."

"Why is it yours?"

"The caravan's full of stuff like this."

"I can't" said Jan.

"Why not?"

"It isn't yours."

"It will be, when I inherit the family fortune."

"No. It's a great idea. But I can't. Find me something. One day. Special. OK?"

"OK." He stood up and went to the door. "Goodbye, house."

"See you tomorrow," said Jan.

Tom shook his head.

"Why not?"

"Crewe."

"What?"

Both their voices were whisper.

"Don't like good-bye. Been good-bye since you told me. Your first Saturday. Crewe."

"I don't leave for nearly a week. Why waste that time?"

"Practice. While there's a safety net. I might not be able to manage. Might not have a head for heights."

"That's plain sick."

"Tom's a-cold."

"I love you."

"I have a gift for self-dramatisation."

"I still love you."

"It's important."

"I know."

"Ten o'clock."

Jan nodded.

"Look at that Milky Way," said Tom. "One hundred

37

thousand million stars. One hundred thousand million specks of dust turning. It's just a steaming poached egg in space."

"You can't have eggs twice," said Jan. "My eyes."

"Galactic."

"Hurt."

"Too full of stars."

He walked home, the Mizpah in his hand. Why did I make Jan cry? I wasn't leaving. This isn't me. He stared at Orion.

It was waiting. It was the waiting. She had stood all morning, watching the men. They were cutting the edge of the Barrow Hill below the graveyard to make a sheer bank. The mire of the Wulvarn gave protection on the lane side. Thomas worked with them, next to Dick Steele, men in slime to their thighs, black all over with falling. She stood at her doorway and felt neither warmth from the hearth nor cold from the air.

John Fowler came riding along the bed of the Wulvarn, not on the lane. He slowed at the Barrow Hill to give news, then went straight to the Rectory. The men worked harder.

Bad news.

There was a shout. She saw Thomas kneeling in the mud, and hurried down the path to the gate, but Dick Steele had waved the men back to their work. Thomas ran, his hands tight against his chest, as if in prayer.

"Madge!" he called. "Madge!"

"What's up? Are you badly?"

"No, no no! Fetch water. I must wash me!"

He stumbled into the house. His fists were a ball of mud. She poured water over his hands into a bowl. The earth fell away. He was holding a smooth shape.

"I found it! I've found one! In the bank! Luck, Madge!"

It was polished, grey-green, and looked like an axe head made of stone. One end was oval, and a hole ran through it, as if for a handle; the other was curved to an edge.

"It fell out of the bank and I caught it. There's not a mark."

"We had lightning, backend. Was it far in?"

"Just below graveyard."

"It looks fresh. It must've been this backend: October."

Thomas washed and dried the stone. The hard weight lay in his hand.

"Fetch us me hammer," he said. "There'll be enough for everyone."

"You're never going to smash it—"

"It's luck. A bit in each chimney, and then. Lightning doesn't hit same place twice."

"How many down there saw?"

"Dick Steele. The others were talking to John. Hey, he was near taken at Crewe, was John. He says they're coming. We need the luck, Madge—"

"Where's the luck in bits of stone? Get scratting in the Wulvarn if it's stones you want."

"I'm master!"

"And I'm saying."

"You'll not stop me!"

"I shall."

"I'll smash it!"

"You won't."

"I will!"

"Who says?"

"I say!"

She put the stone behind her back.

"Give it me! I'm master! Give me that stone!"

"Why?"

"I—I—can—"

"Can what?"

"I can read! I can! John's learning me! So you give that stone here!"

"Read?"

"Yes! And—write. And then he'll learn me Greek, and all sorts, good as Oxford."

"You'll need a calm head for that,' said John. He stood at the door. "What's the noise? It sounded as if

39

they were here already." He was dressed in labourer's clothes.

"I found a thunderbolt on Barrow Hill, and she won't let me smash it," said Thomas.

"Why not, Margery?"

"Would you?" she said. "Feel."

John took the stone and slid his hands over it.

"That wasn't made to be broken, wasn't that," she said.

"What would you do with it?"

"Keep it."

"Thou shalt not make unto thee my graven image, Margery."

"Give over. We hear enough from your father in church, without you starting."

"Back to the lads, Thomas," said John. "I'll be wih you."

"You're wasting your time with that one," said Thomas as he went out. "She'd mither a nest of rats."

John picked up the axe. "I've never seen a thunderstone," he said. His touch flowed over the lines. "It's beautiful."

"Thomas won't hurt it."

"Of course not."

"He wants to help: and it'd make the others think more on him."

"Why shouldn't he? It is luck."

"That's not all it is," said Margery.

"You reckon?"

"Don't you?"

A single bell began to ring over the parish.

"Is it church time already?" said Margery.

"No. My father. He thinks we'll be up against reasonable men."

"Have you seen them?"

"Nearly. I rode down through Crewe by Oak Farm. They'd not left any alive. I must go and stop that bell. They'll find us soon enough."

She wrapped the stone axe in a petticoat and laid it by the chimney.

John smiled. "You know, just for today," he said,

"I could wish you'd married your other Thomas. We've a use for that one now."

"We're well shut of him."

"You were a right pair."

"I married a Rowley, not a Venables."

"Thomas Venables was born fighting."

"Aren't they all on Mow Cop?"

"And you were courting strong."

"So you say."

John walked down the path. Margery went with him.

"Don't let Thomas hear you say Venables."

"He's not jealous!"

"Hadn't you best stop that bell?"

"It can wait," said John. There was smoke over Crewe. "A lot's never been said."

"A lot shouldn't be. I married Thomas Rowley."

"Good."

"Then leave him quiet. Don't work him up with ideas of learning."

"He already knows more than I could learn."

"And don't bait me. You and your reading and that."

"It's what we make do with, if we can't be Thomas Rowley."

"But—books, Latin—"

"The greater part of rubbish."

"But when he's badly—"

"—that man sees God."

"Him? Thomas? Where's God when you're stiff as a plank and your tongue's down your throat?"

John shrugged. "He's not at Barthomley these days, and that's for sure." He crossed the bridge over the Wulvarn, leaving her. "I'm not completed, Madge. I'll say it now. You and I meet in Thomas."

"Bugger off!" Her anger was caught in the swing of the bell, and at its next lull she was empty.

John went into the pulpit. He was dirty and still roughly dressed.

"The Lord be with you," he said.

The people answered, "And with thy spirit."

"Thanks be to God," said John. "Now listen. The Irish have landed. And they're for the King. They've neither clothing, food nor weapons, and they're swinging round Crewe to get them. We stay here and keep our heads down.

"We've water in church, and hens and cattle are being brought from the Rectory. Cooking will be by the tower door. Children will go out to milk cows on empty farms. Lavatories are the north and south chapels. Now the grace of our Lord Jesus Christ, and the love of God, and the fellowship of the Holy Ghost, be with us all evermore."

"Amen."

John left the pulpit.

"What are you gawping at?" said Margery.

"I'm reading," said Thomas.

"The vigil may be long," said the Rector, "but let us, with the psalmist, each ask our Father, 'Be not far from me, for trouble is near and there is none to help. Many bulls encompass me, young bulls of Bashan surround me, they open their mouths at me like a ravening lion.' He will not forsake us at this time of the Nativity. Therefore let us welcome the Christ Child with gladsome hearts, though we be lost sheep among wolves. And if we suffer much, yet shall we be spared. These Irish are but men in a strange land."

"Reading what?" said Margery.

"That carving on chapel screen, where Dick Steele's pissing."

"What's it say, then?"

" 'Let there be no strife: for we be brethren.' "

"How do I know?" she said.

Face stopped behind at Barthomley the next day to burn the huts. He would wait until dark.

The girl walked hobbled, her wrists tied. Macey fed her when they ate. Logan found the route. Magoo covered. They travelled the ten kilometers, and it was evening again before they reached Mow Cop.

Scrub grew high on the mountain, but the ridge was

stone, without shelter. "No fire," said Logan. "Not until we're certain." He sent Magoo to look for a camp
site. "Get us out of the wind."

Macey was quiet from the killing. The girl watched
Logan. The wind would finish them by dawn.

Magoo came back. "It's good," he said. "You'd
think we were expected."

"Occupied?"

"No—well, since we're tribal, I don't like it: but if
we weren't, I'd say we had it made."

"Get us out of this wind," said Logan. "And don't
skyline us."

"It's all skyline," said Magoo.

They climbed among grit slabs to the peak, and
onto a tilted platform that ended in a cliff. The mule
skidded, and Macey had to wedge himself as an an-
chor.

"There," said Magoo.

"I don't know what it is," said Logan, "but I'm not
asking."

There was a recess in the platform, as if a cube had
been picked out of the rock. It was twenty feet deep,
and a path went down one of the walls.

"Tent for now," said Logan. "We can roof over
when we're settled."

"If you go in, you'll die," said the girl.

"Sweetheart, I've been in," said Magoo.

"You'll die."

"What will she mean?" said Logan.

"It's an old quarry, or something. No recent working. Don't worry: I'll fix this one."

Magoo pushed the girl down the path. She fell, and
he maimed her as she lay.

"You've done nothing to me," she said. "There's no
pain. I'm not hurt."

"Shurrup," said Magoo.

Logan and Macey took the first watch. In the night
a fire showed. "Barthomley," said Logan. "Face'd better make the most of it: he'll be a while before he's
that warm again."

Macey pulled his cloak around the weight of his shoulder. "She needs bandages," he said.

"Magoo's job."

"She won't let him."

"Her problem: but if it bothers you—don't be long."

"We're all mates."

"She isn't," said Logan.

Macey turned to go. He screamed, threw himself backwards, scrabbling at the rock. Logan choked him with an elbow and kicked his sword away.

"They—they're—don't make me! They're—not there! They're not there! My mates! All! There's nothing!"

"Get down!" Logan swore at him.

Magoo appeared out of the shelter, armed. "What's up?"

"Macey. Give us a hand."

"Come on, you prannock," said Magoo. "Get down them steps."

"No. No steps. Nothing."

"Get bleeding down!"

"Height!" Macey opened his mouth, and through Logan's full strength a cry broke, one sound, rising in pitch. Magoo hit behind the ear, and Macey collapsed. They dragged him into the tent.

"He was for going again," said Logan. "I could feel it in him. Why?"

"You're the expert in his little ways," said Magoo.

"He's never been like this; until he killed that guard."

"Happen it's that," said Magoo. "Let's have a look." He reached for Macey's shoulder.

"No," said Logan. "The order stands. Nobody to touch him."

"Of course, sir. I was forgetting."

"Take watch. Don't call me 'sir'."

The wind made their teeth ache.

"Some Ninth you'd have," said Magoo, "if you'd killed me for frisking Macey, and the rest of our mob didn't make it from Barthomley."

44

"We'd manage."

"I don't see you as Officer in Charge of one nutter and a slag."

"She'd breed."

"But how long can you go it up here?"

"For ever."

"Roll on, winter."

"Give over," said Logan. "Check me on Mother's dialect. It's a while till light."

They settled in their positions.

" 'Stream,' " said Magoo.

" 'Beck.' "

" 'Valley.' "

" 'Dale.' "

" 'Field' or 'yard.' "

" 'Garth.' "

" 'Cold.' "

" 'Starved.' "

" 'Hungry.' "

" 'Clemmed.' "

" 'Fed up.' "

"—'Mithered'?"

"That's Cat."

" 'Agait.' "

"No."

"Tell me," said Logan.

" 'Borsant.' "

"I'm right borsant, starved and fair clemmed on this cop," said Logan.

"Not bad," said Magoo.

Face reached scrub line after dawn. He hung back until Logan whistled.

"Go and see if Macey's come round, and if he has, tell him to fix breakfast."

"She can do that," said Magoo.

Face climbed the slabs.

"Barthomley?" said Logan.

"No trouble."

"Good. We're settling in. We've got it made. What do you think of that?"

Face looked at the square hole in the rock. "Get the hell out of there, Logan, or you're dead."

"It was the waiting."

"It was."

They stood on the platform. A line of trolleys rattled by, and people moved, but Tom and Jan held each other invisible.

"Checking."

"What?"

"Memory: hair in my face."

"You."

"And you."

"It was waiting."

They had to step back to be closer.

"Let me look at you," said Tom.

"You're too far away."

"Your fault."

They came together again.

"Are your eyes shut?"

"Yes."

"Funny. I shut my eyes to be with you when I'm not, and when I am——"

"You shut them!"

They giggled, and went the length of Crewe station, skipping, running, breaking to rejoin, under the glass, the dark bridge and into the daylight to the platform's tip, and back again. The platform made a headland above the woven lines, and at the end, away from passengers, was an old bench. Tom and Jan sat there in the sunlight and wind and watched the junction.

"Like Blackpool prom, isn't it?"

"Quieter."

"Coffee?" said Jan.

"Yes."

They returned to the gloom and announcements and people, trains drawing hands apart.

"Don't look," said Tom.

They sat in the cafeteria and drank their coffee.

"So I may switch to a medical degree," said Jan. "I can't see myself as Matron."

"I thought the glamour wouldn't last."

"The first bedpan! No, I'll do the two years for experience, but I think I'd like to follow up Mum and Dad."

"They sold 'The Limes.'"

"How is it?"

"I've not been."

"You've still got the key?"

"Sure."

"Dad says will you give it to the new people."

"I'll drop it in next week. Can we go somewhere else now?"

"What's wrong?"

"This room's empty."

"It's full!"

"But no one's here," said Tom. "Let's go. Please."

They went up the steps and through the barrier. The road was noisy and there was grit in the wind.

"Where?" said Jan.

"Into town. I'm panicked on stations. I don't know that anybody's real."

"You've not changed, have you?"

"No."

"Good!"

The town was busy. Tom and Jan walked with the crowd. There was a current of movement through the terraced streets.

"With stations," said Tom, "you'd find it hard to prove that it wasn't full of ghosts."

"I bet that's not original."

"Nothing I say is."

"I love you," said Jan.

"Get that for innovation!"

"This must be the middle," said Jan. "The traffic's going round in circles." They were at a shopping precinct.

"It's far enough," said Tom: "and parky. Let's have a warm."

He took Jan's arm and led her into a furniture shop.

It was sombre with rolled carpets on end. Kitchens were laid out for breakfast. Tom stepped between the carpets into the window display of three-piece suites and sat down in deep chintz. He pulled Jan next to him and stretched his legs to the glass where the fire would have been. He smiled in the spotlights.

"You're showing off," said Jan.

"In comfort, though. And if you keep your voice down we shan't be noticed. They're not bothered in the street, are they? I've brought sandwiches." He took a packet from his anorak and unwrapped it on the carpet. "Spam," he said. "And banana."

"Mind the floor."

"The maids will clear."

They ate the sandwiches, cupping their hands to catch crumbs.

"Not my father's, I'm afraid."

"I miss him. Those Sunday teas."

"He is strangely civilised."

"How's your mother?"

"She misses him, too: if he's quick."

"Idiot." Jan gathered up the remains of the food.

"He's a good cook," said Tom.

"Is that all?"

"Take your coat off. You'll feel the cold if you don't."

They nestled in the sofa. The crowd shopped, passed by.

"I'm beginning to wonder if we're here," said Tom.

"Your mother's written to me once or twice."

"She never said." He unclipped a price ticket and fastened it to his jeans. "Do you think they'll believe in us now? I'm Twenty Guineas To Clear. What'll you be? An Uncut Moquette?"

"You're crackly. Why?"

"I think our taste is lacking. That rug isn't quite us. But then this can never be a room for anybody else. We're bits of other futures."

"What is it?"

"Crackly. Spiders under my skin."

"Why?"

"Because I'm out of my mind for you, and the instant you step off that train it's the beginning of parting. Time runs out on us. I'm not living. I'm one Crewe station. I wake each morning hoping the day's the dream and the night real. You don't send letters very often—"

"I do—"

"—and I'm so futile and lonely and miserable and awash with self-pity without you, and I've no money, and I've ridden sixteen miles on my mother's bike to get here, and we sit in this public privacy, and it's what I live for, it's the real time, but as soon as we reach it, it starts to go and all our living and working and doing is apart and time-between, and if this is what it's like after eight weeks—"

"Can I help you, sir?" asked a salesman.

"I doubt it."

"Can I help you?"

"You might, if you didn't ask rhetorical questions."

"Thank you," said Jan. "We're going."

"There was no need for me to be rude to that man, either," said Tom on the pavement. The wind gusted his white face.

"I haven't waited all this time, and come all this way, to be miserable," said Jan in the British Home Stores.

"I'm sorry."

"You always are."

"I see everything at once."

"Try not to be so clever, for a change. Be more positive. Nothing's ever wasted. When we're apart, think of the next time getting nearer."

"Yes, nurse."

"The bottle's half full, not half empty."

"It used to be up to the neck and brimming over."

"It still is, if you think straight."

"This cafeteria's a cattle-pen."

"I'll thump you."

"Still, it's not bad. In evolutionary terms, Olduvai Gorge to Crewe in two million years is knocking on."

"And you are changing the subject."

49

"No. Your argument is impeccable. My attitude was negative."

"Why do you give in without a fuss?"

"When you're wrong, and rumbled, it's better to be the first to say so."

"That's still dodging the issue."

"I know."

They moved from shop to shop, resting for as long as they were unnoticed, until they found a crowded Bingo room, so busy and full of smoke that they were able to sit in peace. They watched whole families ranged intent on their illuminated panels, while prams and children rolled about the floor.

"Parents' Day at Cape Kennedy," said Tom. "Watch their concentration."

"All over nothing."

"There's something to be said for random selection in a causal universe." Tom was looking at the coloured numbered balls as they danced in the air jet before being sucked into choice. "You and I met with as much reason."

The Bingo litany was intoned through loudspeakers.

"That woman has a lump of coal in front of her," said Jan.

"Why not?"

"It's primitive! She's behaving as though talismans change things."

"Perhaps they do."

"A lump of coal?"

"There may be a fossil in it," said Tom.

The day went.

They walked back towards the station in the early dark.

"Have you remembered Orion? Ten o'clock?"

"Every night," said Jan. "The girls must think I'm barmy."

"It'll be well up by the time you reach Euston." He bought a platform ticket. "I've been thinking about what you said. There are no good-byes, are there? As soon as the train comes. I'll not wait. The train's the beginning of meeting."

50

"Yes."

"Smile, then."

The train snaked across the points. Tom opened a door.

"Hello," he said.

"Hello."


"Is not my word like a fire? saith the Lord; and like a hammer that breaketh the rock in pieces—"

"I should've smashed it," said Thomas. "Rector's telling me."

"You big lummox," said Margery. "He's talking about the Irish."

"Let us pray," said the Rector.

"There wanted a Temper, and Thou wast the cause that he was wanting. There wanted time and place, and Thou wast the cause that they wanted. The Tempter was present, and there wanted neither places nor time, but Thou heldest me back, that I should not consent.

"The Tempter came full of darkness, as he is, and Thou didest harden me, that I might despise him.

"The Tempter came armed and strongly, but to the intent he should not overcome me, Thou didest restrain him and strengthen me.

"The Tempter came transformed into an Angel of Light, and to the intent he should not deceive me, Thou didest rebuke him, and to the intent I should know him thou didest enlighten me.

"For he is the great red dragon, the old serpent—"

"Eh up," said Margery, "he's not taken breath yet."

"—which draweth down the third part of the stars of Heaven with his tail, and casteth them to the gound—"

"Mister Fowler," said Dick Steele, "you'll not mind if we get on, will you?"

"You must do as you please," said the Rector.

"I doubt prayers won't keep muskets off, and there's that bank to be finished yet."

"You're welcome in this church," said the Rector. "But leave the dead to their rest."

"There's none as'll worry if they're thrutched before doomsday."

"If you're for war, send to the garrison at Crewe."

"They know already," said John. "But do you think they'd come? And if they did?"

"A horse eats its share, choose what the rider's coat," said Dick Steele.

"It's all one to me," said Randal Hassall. "It doesn't matter what a man calls his bloody self when he's taking my cows. They've still bloody went."

"They trample us," said John.

" 'Us'?" said the Rector.

"They've trampled, and spoilt—and they'll not do it again."

"Thatch burns without taking sides, Rector."

"Mine bloody did. Twice. Once for King, once for Parliament. And no bloody harvest, neither."

"I have called you here for safety," said the Rector. "The Irish are starved and naked, with years of fighting in their bellies. We are not their concern. Is it not better to lose food and cloth than life and house and land? Show Christmas in our hearts."

"The prayer you started," said John. "Doesn't it end, 'But Thou, O Lord, deliver us from the net of the Fowler'?"

"That's bloody telling him."

"Watch your tongue, Mister," the Rector said to John. "Especially in the company you've chosen."

"You reckon?"

" 'Those who refuse to rule must be ruled by those inferior to themselves,' " the Rector said in Greek.

" 'But who will rule the rulers?' " John answered in Latin.

"I like to hear old church talk again," said Jim Boughey. "Services aren't what they were now we understand them."

"Go back to sleep," said John. "Dick, we'll leave the bank. Set watch from the tower. Margery, help with the women. Thomas, fetch the cows by the North Door and tether them. Settle down. Clear two rows of

52

pews for firewood, but mind the rushes don't catch. Father—if you've prayers—I'm sorry—"

The Rector looked down from the pulpit. "I've prayers," he said. "And faith. What more can you achieve?"

"Whatever I will to do," said John.

"Oh?" The Rector's voice was cold. "'Can you bind the chains of the Pleiades, or loose the cords of Orion?'"

"That's Job thirty-eight thirty-one. But I'll find my own words. You say your prayers."

"Cop hold of this," said Margery. She gave Thomas a bundle from under her shawl. "And don't you harm it while I get back."

"Right, Madge."

Sparks echoed, and a thin line of smoke strung to the roof. Thomas packed the bundle inside his shirt, opened the North Door and brought in the cows from the graveyard. Children were beginning to organise their games. The men of the watch who were not on the tower played dice by the spiral stair. John moved among the groups. The smell of living filled the church.

"It's her petticoat," said Thomas, pleased and furtive as he opened his shirt for John to look. "From when we were handseled. We went getting alder bark all along the Wulvarn one Sunday for dye it."

"Keep it safe, then, you heathen," said John. "And the thunderstone. She's set a lot by both, think on. Don't smash it."

"The lesson is taken from the sixtieth book of Isaiah," said the Rector, "beginning to read at the first verse. 'Arise, shine; for your light has come, and the glory of the Lord has risen upon you. For behold, darkness shall cover the earth, and thick darkness the peoples.'"

"I'd not smash it. Not now. Really. Not with the petticoat and that."

"You're fond, Thomas Rowley. Let's be doing."

"Any mail?"

"Aunty Evelyn and Uncle Peter, Aunty Marina,

Mr. and Mrs. Harrison: one from London. Father'll be home shortly. And I don't want you in the kitchen. It'll spoil the treat."

"I'll revise my Greek," said Tom. He lay on his bed and put the cans over his ears.

The caravan dipped as Tom's father came up the steps from the carport. He was holding a square box against his chest. Tom felt his parents move about the kitchen. He gave them five minutes, then closed his book.

"Ready?" he said.

"Yes."

He went into the kitchen. They were sitting at the table.

" '—Happy Birthday, dear To-hom;

" 'Happy Birthday to you!' "

He looked at the cake in the middle of the table. "Did you make that?"

"Is it all right?" said his father.

"It's incredible."

The cake was the shape of a railway engine, the icing meticulous and coloured, with his father's regimental crest on the side.

"Do you like it?"

"It's—"

"I was plundering my mind for a theme," said his father, "a motif: I thought we needed to show—"

"It's—"

"—We needed to show you were going far."

"It's great."

"He thinks a lot of you," said Tom's mother. "You don't like it, do you?"

"It must have taken ages—"

"Oh, an hour here and there—"

"He was up all times last week. Didn't come home till three this morning."

"Thanks," said Tom. "Thanks very much. Thanks."

"Presents next," said his mother.

"We didn't know what to give you—"

"They're only odds and ends—"

"You shouldn't have bothered—"

54

"And you're growing so fast—"

"Am I?"

"We couldn't think—"

"Anyway—"

"It's all right," said Tom.

"Well, open them."

The first packet was a tie and two pairs of socks.

"You can change them if they're no use."

"No. They're great. Thanks."

"Or I'll have 'em," said his father.

"You won't!" said Tom. He unfastened his mother's present. It was a notebook with a padded binding, and the title in gold leaf: "Books I Have Read."

"It's got columns for Dates, Names and Comments," said his mother.

"Yes. Yes. Smashing. Thanks."

"That's all," said his father. "We didn't know what would do for, for, well, what you might call a real present."

"Don't worry," said Tom.

"But we're getting one: later, like."

"Actually," said Tom, "the money would do."

"It would not!" said his mother. "You'd only spend it."

"It's like gift tokens," said his father. "There's no thought behind them."

"We're saving up," said his mother. "You'll have a special one for Christmas."

"Now then." His father cleared the wrapping paper away. He folded each piece, and arranged the presents either side of the cake, propping the book against a plate. Buns, trifle, jam tarts and two different flavors of jelly: and lemonade. "Now then." He checked the camera. "Pretend to cut the cake. Ready? Hold it."

Flash.

"One more."

Tom sat and looked at the table. "I'm very grateful—"

"Of course, love," said his mother. "Now have some trifle. It's your favourite."

"What's Janet sent?" said his father.

"A card."

"No present?" said his mother.

"We'd arranged—"

"Nursing's not well salaried," said his father. "It's more what you might call a vocation."

"She'll have means."

"She's living off her pay," said Tom.

"Still, she might've sent something," said his mother. "She could afford to go wherever it was she went this year."

"Parcel post's often delayed—"

"Give over," said Tom's mother. "Can't you see you're upsetting him?"


"When did the god come to you?" she said.

"Did he?" said Macey.

He sat with her by the fire. She painted him again with alder. Autumn was over. Logan had made them build huts among the crags, empty deployments of strength. No tribe had been seen, and in that time they had grown their hair, and tattooed their skins, to cover the sear of armour.

"The god attacked Barthomley in you, and you couldn't be killed."

"I'm outside when Macey's killing."

"Then the god is in you."

"Not any more."

She marked his brow with the red juice. "What god is he?"

"I don't remember. My father wasn't told to me. Only the axe. I was seven when the Romans came, and I lay by a chariot while the huts were burning, and I looked at the flames in the thatch through the spokes. The wheel was going round— Then I was in a Roman tent. They said I'd killed eleven men. Logan stopped me. That's how it's been. I can't fight. He knows about the axe. Sometimes Logan makes me go. Macey kills. That's why they keep him. He's good at it."

"Close your eyes."

He nestled and reached for her ear. "That's what I want."

"Feel safe?"

"Safer."

"Still scared?"

He burrowed against her.

"What of?"

"Same. Blue silver. And red. And. And the thing I see."

"Tell me," she said. "Don't be scared."

"Sometimes. When I'm on watch, and I'm scared, and blue silver—there's no camp—just empty—no you. No you. Edge of the rock, I see—a tower. It scares me. Are you scared?"

"I'm not the one who has to see it."

"There's more. When I went blue silver at Barthomley, I saw a tower among the huts on the grave mound. There was a door in the tower, and I ran to hide from Macey while he was killing. I ran through a big door, into a stone forest, very dark, but sun shining down between the trees, all different colours, and I know it was night. But Macey wasn't killing. I was. I killed your men under the tower in the stone forest, but there wasn't one."

"What else? You killed the men: why shouldn't the rest be true?"

"Things."

"What things?"

"All sorts. I can't tell you. Things. No names. Things. Not real. Never before. Are they? These things. I see."

"Close your eyes," she said. "Forget about them."

"You don't believe me."

"I do believe you. We're the ones who can't see. Happen we're lucky. Why does the blue silver come?"

"Dunno. It came. When. I killed the man. I use the axe. Macey doesn't kill him. Macey doesn't kill him. Macey's gone away. I'm scared. Axe and Macey don't like me killing. They leave me. But I can't look after my mates. I need Macey and stone axe."

"Are they your mates?"

"All. All brilliant. They look after me. They look after Macey."

"Do you like them?"

"They're my mates."

"Aren't you angry? What they did. Their child. In me."

He shook. "That follows killing."

"Mend what's broken?"

"I can't mend stone axe."

"You'll find a way."

"How?"

"You'll know."

"Happen they'll not keep me, when they find I'm no use, when they find Macey's gone."

She smiled. "Happen."

Logan entered the hut. "There's a gang on the cop, with mules. What's it about?"

"They'll not attack," she said.

Face came in. "You've left nothing in that rock hole, have you?" he said to Logan.

"No."

"If they think we've been in there—" Face turned on the girl. "One word from you and I'll slit your throat, OK? Logan, you stay inside. You wouldn't pass for tribal yet. We'll scare them off, Magoo and me. Macey—out. Look sharp."

"They'll not attack," she said.

"Think on," said Face. "I've got your number. You don't fool me."

Magoo whistled from the crag, and Face ran to him.

The girl dragged herself across the floor. "Lift me to a bench," she said. "Fetch me a cloak." Logan and Macey helped her up. "Both of you," she said, "don't speak."

Magoo and Face watched the men approach along the ridge.

"There's five," said Magoo. "We could pick them off. What've they come for?"

"Religious," said Face. "It had to be some time."

58

"If we let them too close they'll know we're under-strength."

"What would Mothers do if they had something another tribe wanted?"

"Keep it."

"But if the Mothers didn't want it?"

"Still keep it."

"But if they didn't want a war on their hands, like we don't want to take on the whole of Cheshire right now?"

"You reckon?"

"We've got to do a deal with those five and still give them the runaround."

"I say we knock 'em off."

"We don't kill anybody: not on this mountain."

"What are they after?"

"Millstones. From that hole. They'll do anything to get them; but they won't want a fight. The protection works both ways."

"Then that's the deal. Protection."

"How do we set it up?"

"Nobody argues with a Mother."

"Can you bluff?"

"Watch me."

Magoo stood clear on the skyline. The men halted.

"Now then," said Magoo. "Off this garth."

One of the Cats came forward and held his arms open. "We've only hammers and chisels and some pinchbars," he said.

The other men unrolled wolfe pelts and set down bags of grain. "For the quarry," said the Cat.

Magoo glanced sideways at Face.

"And you'll let us speak to Barthomley?" said the Cat.

"Eh up," said Face. "Don't push this. It's more than it looks."

Logan had fired the kindling in all the huts, and put glass on to make smoke. The settlement was occupied.

"You and one other bring the gear. The rest stay where you are," said Magoo. "And watch them: don't let them too near Logan," he said to Face. "I'll stay here."

Face took the men to the hut. Macey sat outside, his skin dyed red. The men avoided him.

Inside the hut the girl was waiting. Logan had found the darkest shadow, away from light and fire.

The Cat knelt before her. "How do?" he said.

"The goddess does well," she replied.

"Stick to the point," said Face.

"We're from Bosley. Does the goddess allow stone?"

"She does."

"Is the stone pure?"

"It will be."

"The sacrifices—"

"—will be made."

"There is a redman. Where did he kill?"

"Barthomley."

"We have brought rye."

"It is needed."

"Has the goddess her stone?"

"She has."

"How does it grind?"

"Sun-rising."

The Cat left the hut. He stopped by Macey, but did not look at him. "May the god pass from you," he said.

Macey sat still.

The Cat came back to the doorway of the hut. "Congratulations sergeant-major," he said in Latin. "You sure made a swell job of these guys."

Face ran.

"They're down in that pit," said Magoo.

"I'll tell you something else," said Face. "They know who we are, what we are, and you can bet they know how many we are."

"I thought it was too bloody quiet. Let's get the buggers now. They're sitting ducks."

"We daren't risk it. This is their holy mountain, and that quarry's the centre."

"That's why no attacks."

"I don't like it."

"The tribute's good."

"Very. Furs for winter, and enough rye till spring: like they were cultivating us."

"What was with the girl?"

"She's a corn goddess, and as long as they think she's OK—"

"Uh-huh."

"I guessed it when we found her. She'd all the signs And she'll have a few more by spring—and that might not be too healthy."

"So where's it leave us?"

"On a bloody cold cop."

The Cats worked all day in the quarry, cutting stone into shallow blocks which they loaded on the mules. They sang as they worked, and poured beer on the mountain as each piece was prised loose. Magoo watched.

Logan sat outside the hut with Face. "They'd probably know the day we moved in. All this pantomime for nothing."

Face stabbed the earth with a knife. "And they've not tried us."

"Any ideas?"

"The girl. Or we're some use. But no feuding for Barthomley: and they let us stay on their mountain. It doesn't figure. I reckon we sit tight through winter, and then move somewheres come spring. If they let us, and we don't antagonise."

"All that tribal, and they knew—"

"Better still keep to it," said Face.

"Yeh. But I feel such a twat."

"They're cleaning up and going," Magoo called. "They're washing the frigging place now."

"Hey! What's Macey doing?"

Macey had taken a sword and was waving it over his head.

"I'll save you! Save my mates! All my brilliant mates! Kill the Cats! Kill the Cats! Watch me flip!"

He ran towards them. The mules were strung along the cop ridge, headed for Bosley.

"That's not for real," said Logan. "Kid! Come back!"

"Kill the Cats! Brilliant mates!"

He was jumping, shaking the sword. The Cats paused. He danced around them, screamed at them. They ignored him. Then he was too far from the huts and he halted like a lost dog, and came puling down the slope. Magoo caught his sword and tripped him as he passed. Macey sprawled and rolled down to the huts. Logan and Face picked him up and slung him inside. He grabbed at the girl, and she held him.

"Don't act stupid, kid," Face had never seen such an expression in Logan's eyes. There was pain. "Don't play soldiers." He spoke to Face. "The kid's finished. Some Ninth!"

Logan shook the girl. "What's this place? Why come here for rocks?"

She did not let go of Macey.

"What's so special about Mow Cop?" Logan shouted.

"It's the netherstone of the world," she said. "The skymill turns on it to grind stars."

"Why haven't we been attacked?"

"The rock is sacred to the flour of heaven."

Magoo clattered across the slope. He was out of breath, excited, and came to the hut swinging a weight. He threw it along the floor, and the weight fell apart as human heads.

"As soon as they stepped off their precious mountain," said Magoo.

"What the hell are you on?" said Logan.

"We're Mothers, aren't we?"

"They know we're not!"

"They know different now."

"There were five. There's only four here."

"Yes, well, we always let one go—to prove what's happened to the rest."

"They cared so much. They really cared."

"Didn't you know?" said Jan.

"But it wasn't me they cared about. It was Little

62

Boy's Birthday. Lemonade: every time lemonade. And then my mother started sniping at you for not sending anything except the card."

"Bicker bicker bicker bicker bicker," said Jan. "You're as bad as them. Anyway, I've brought you a present."

"But we were saving—"

"I said 'brought,' not 'bought.' Come on."

They had met outside the barrier at Crewe, to avoid paying for a platform ticket. Jan took him by the arm and walked away from the station.

"What is it?" said Tom.

"I've decided, for your birthday, not to let you indulge yourself. We're going to enjoy every minute."

"I was sounding off, that's all."

"Then do it at the caravan, not here."

The smoky Bingo room was the same, the same people: the balls danced like atoms to coincide with numbers on the bright panels.

Frost had come early. The last warmth of the sun was killed by mist. Tom and Jan moved around the shops. The best heaters were over the door of Marks and Spencer, and there was colour in the Fine Fare supermarket, but it was hard to stay private. The mirrors were observant.

"Happy?" said Jan.

"Very."

"Me too."

"Living apart, so broke we can't eat, moaned at by parents, hanging about shop doorways to keep warm in the last town God made, and totally happy."

The ceiling tinkled with music and persuasions to buy.

"You know what Crewe is?" said Tom. "Ultimate reality. That's why we can't touch it. Each of these shops is full of every aspect of one part of existence. Woolworth's is a tool shed; Boots, a bathroom; the British Home Stores, a wardrobe. And we walk through it all, but we can't clean our teeth, or mend a fuse, or change our socks. You'd starve in this supermarket. It's all so real, we're shadows."

"Care for a brisk walk before lunch?"

"But do you understand?"

"Of course I don't. That's why I love you."

"Am I really worth the journey?"

"Idiot—"

"And the hysteria, and the portable caravan?"

"You're just fishing for compliments now."

"If you knew—Never mind."

"Men! Why can't you accept that we're very lucky and happy, against the odds, and leave it at that?"

"There are so many pressures."

"But as long as we're us, they only make the bridge stronger. Think: we were made by love, for love."

"By love, for love."

"Yes!"

"You know that."

"Yes!"

"That's the difference."

"What difference?"

"Not all of it applies to me. I wish to God it did. Tom's a-cold."

"I know the remedy."

"So do I."

"A brisk walk!" said Jan.

They set off at random. Away from the precinct the terraces became all the town, and the roads were full of noise.

"This is better," said Jan. They had crossed a railway bridge onto a piece of quiet land between houses. A boy on a bicycle overtook them and disappeared at the opposite corner of the space. "There's a way through."

The path ran down to another street, but facing them was a break in the terraces. Two gables almost touched.

"I wonder why they don't," said Tom.

There was room to pass, and beyond they came to an open square, backed by houses.

"Most peculiar—"

From the square the path continued, cobbled, and overgrown by hedges that met in a tunnel arch.

"That's old," said Tom. "Older than Crewe."

The path dropped steeply through silence to a bridge across a river, rising beyond. Each time it met a road, there was a way, beckoning further, along gaps and entries.

"If you kept to the streets, you'd never see this," said Tom. "It always cuts at right angles, same as the alleys."

Sometimes it was as wide as a road, though only children seemed to own it, but even their games were muted.

"Have you any idea where we are?" said Jan.

"I'm more uneasy about the 'when.' "

But the path was stopped.

"Fairly definite," said Jan. "Shall we have lunch after our brisk walk?"

They were looking over a fence and across the marshalling yards, sidings and main lines of Crewe.

"No." Tom climbed the fence. "It's older than railways."

"Come back!"

He was picking his way among the tracks towards the distant trees on the far side.

"It's dangerous!"

He moved as if on a scent, and she had to follow him over the steel. Points snapped blindly, without cause or warning: there was no place to hide, and trains were everywhere, and it was impossible to know which line they would be on. High pylons carried rows of lamps.

"Tom!"

"I am in blood stepped in so far—"

An express came between them.

"—Returning were as tedious as go o'er!"

"Sod Shakespeare! It's us!"

She caught up with him.

"You're not funny. Those points—If you get your feet clogged—"

"We're more than halfway," said Tom. "It really is the quickest. And can we move a bit faster? There are some gentlemen about three hundred metres away trying to attract our attention."

"Do you wonder?"

"I can't have you fraternising with strangers." Tom smiled. "And I was also right." They had reached the other side, and a path led into open country. "Let's see where this goes, and then have lunch. You did say a brisk walk."

"I didn't mean an assault course."

"There's one thing about Crewe. It knows when to stop."

"Which is more than you do."

The change was precise. They were in deep farmland. The frost had cut the leaves, and they were falling with autumn. There was no town, simply the path.

"Are you angry?" said Tom.

"No. I was scared."

"Sorry. Mind if we go on—see where it ends?"

"But it could be anywhere! Hull!"

"Within reason, then."

"Whose reason?"

"Yours."

She laughed, and put her arms around him.

"This is more like."

"More open," said Tom. "I don't mind the shops and the crowds: they don't touch us."

"I wish we'd some money, though: enough to manage on."

"You wait till I'm rich."

"Shall I?"

The path broke into hedgerows and lanes, but the way was there.

"How's your stamina?" said Tom.

"Great. I could walk for ever."

"If we don't reach the end, we'll stop an hour before we need to turn back, so we don't have to rush."

They walked through undulating country, golden with light from the cold sun.

"That's where I'd like to try for, one day," said Jan.

"I see it from the train, and then I know you're near. It looks like a lonely old man sitting there."

66

"We'll go," said Tom. "But I doubt if it'll be today, unless you feel like running."

"Is it a castle?"

"A folly. Not real. It's called Mow Cop."

"I like mountains. Can we go, even if it is only a folly?"

"Sure. I said. But how about something closer for today?"

Across the fields a red sandstone church tower stood from a valley. The landscape was quiet, scattered farms of black timber, and the lane leading towards the church.

"I bet the path ends there," said Jan.

"It does for now. I'm hungry."

They arrived at the village boundary. A sign was re-emerging from the hedge as the year's growth died.

" 'Barthomley,' " said Jan.

"I don't believe it."

"It's idyllic."

"A *Come to Britain* poster."

The church was on a long, tapered mound that was bigger than the graveyard. The mound butted into the lane. Below the church were a few cottages and a thatched inn. A shallow stream ran by the lane, and was crossed by a footbridge to the only shop.

" 'Saint Bertoline,' " Tom read. "I've not heard of him. Let's see what he has to offer."

They went through the tower door. The church was empty and big. They wandered about, examining the memorials.

"The central heating's efficient," said Tom. "And I'm famished."

They sat in a pew and divided the sandwiches.

"What is it this week?"

"Banana and Spam. I thought I'd ring the changes."

"What's that other soggy?"

"My birthday cake. I saved the last piece for you."

He unwrapped the driver's cab of the railway engine.

"You shouldn't laugh at your father. It's a fantastic compliment—all that careful work."

67

"I don't laugh at him."

"You were trying pretty hard."

"I wasn't laughing."

"You were making him cheap."

"I wasn't"

"You were."

"Let there be no strife," said Tom, "for we be brethren."

"I suppose that's Shakespeare, too."

"Genesis thirteen."

"How do I know?" she said.

"It's carved on the screen right in front of you."

"I love you," she said, "and this cake's good."

"Tom's a-cold."

"Fancy warming this church for nobody," said Tom. "I bet it's empty all week."

"Pick up your crumbs. The church is warmed for somebody—us."

"Space, peace and you," said Tom. "That's all I ask."

"Here we are."

"But we'll have to go soon."

"It'll still be here."

"Can we come next time?"

"Not if we have to cross those sidings!"

"Can we come? It's so big, and quiet, and we can talk. No fuss. Together."

"I'd like it."

"What about Christmas?"

"I've volunteered for duty. The girls chip in a bit if someone doesn't mind staying. It lessens the odds for them. We might be able to have an extra day on it."

"But no presents. Every penny goes towards this. Right?"

"Right. And Mow Cop."

"If we can."

A door opened, and air moved in the church, making small sounds that echoed.

"Who's this?" said Tom. "Saint Bert?"

The Rector, tall, thin, silver-haired, small in the

emptiness, walked down the aisle. He stopped when he saw Tom and Jan.

"Good—afternoon," he said.

"Good afternoon," said Jan.

"What are you doing?"

"Sitting in your church," said Tom.

"Ah. Good."

"Is it all right? I mean, are we interrupting?"

"No. No. Not at all." The Rector's voice was mild, but his face was red.

"I'm sorry if we made you jump," said Tom.

"What were you doing?"

"Talking."

"Ah."

"Aren't you used to finding people here?"

"I suppose it's in order," said the Rector. "Talking: yes. You were talking—"

"Yes, we were," said Jan.

"Ah."

"We were sitting quietly, talking." Jan's voice rose.

"A problem nowadays—"

"Who is?"

"We were very impressed by the water stoup by the North Door," said Tom. "And the tympanum on the exterior of the chancel."

The Rector looked at Tom as if for the first time.

"But, if I may say so, the execution of the Flight into Egypt on the south panel of the altar is one of the finest pieces of Tudor carving in my experience. The vernacular detail is delightful. I would hazard a guess that the font cover is of the same period."

"What is your college?" said the Rector. "Mine is Caius."

"I haven't gone up yet," said Tom. "It's a choice between three at the moment."

"Ah"

"I notice that you keep the South Chapel locked," said Tom. "We were hoping to examine the Fulleshurst monuments."

"Well, you see, one has such problems these days,"

said the Rector. "I'm afraid the keys are at the Rectory. Perhaps next time."

"Of course," said Tom.

"Do call."

"We shall."

"Would it disturb you if I said Evensong?"

"Not at all."

"You're welcome to participate."

"I'm afraid we have to go very shortly."

"Perhaps another time," said the Rector. He genuflected to the east, and began to address the church from the chancel steps.

"When the wicked man turneth away from his wickedness that he hath committed, and doeth that which is lawful and right, he shall save his soul alive.

"Dearly beloved—"

Tom and Jan left the church.

"They always make it dirty! They always try!" Jan stamped up and down outside at the foot of the tower. "They always try to make it dirty! I even feel dirty!"

Tom comforted her. "No. He was a bit thrown when he found there was a congregation."

"Always!—And what was that you baffled him with, for Christ's sake?"

"Please don't use words loosely," said Tom, and held her as her exasperation flared. "It was just an academic trick. Jargon."

"But how did you know all that?"

"I flipped through the pamphlet on the table as we went in."

"He thought! He did! He thought we—!"

"He doesn't now," said Tom. "Which is all that matters. He doesn't equate architecture with immorality."

"We weren't being immoral!"

"I know," said Tom. "And now he knows."

"You're always so tolerant with strangers. Even that furniture salesman. You savage the people near you."

"Perhaps it's to do with open scholarships and closed caravans."

They left Barthomley, and walked back to Crewe by road. It was dark when they reached the town.

"I'm sorry I blew my top," said Jan. "It's not spoilt the church for us, has it?"

"Of course it hasn't."

The library was still open. Tom went to the reference section and found the tithe map. Hardly any of Crewe had been built when it was drawn, and he was able to trace the line of a path crossing the fields.

"There's the river, and the cobbled tunnel's a road, see, going to that square which has the houses backing on it now. Look, it used to be the yard to Oak Farm."

"Nothing else in sight. Out in the wilds. And now."

"I told you the path was special."

"It all was."

"Even the sidings."

"Especially the sidings!"

"I've had a marvellous birthday," Tom said at the barrier.

"Hello, then."

"Hello."


John came up to relieve Randal Hassall on the tower.

"Where are they?"

"There's fires, across from Basford, and coming this way."

"If my father's right, they could be nearer," said John. "We've pulled everybody in, so if they're not burning empty dwellings they could be nearer."

"You're not going bloody soft, are you?"

"No. We stick. After Oak Farm—"

"Good lad."

"Eat something," said John. "There's beef ready."

"We could smell it. That stair's like a bloody chimney."

"Send Dick to relieve Thomas in an hour."

Randal moved his head, as if he wanted to speak. Thomas was leaning over the tower wall, his musket aimed.

71

"What?" said John.

"Him. He's quiet. Not a bloody word. He's not shifted since I don't know when. Reckons he's taking on a bloody army, by the looks of him."

"He'd like to be some help. Leave him."

"He's neither use nor ornament. I'd watch that one."

"I shall."

"I'll go and have baggin, then."

"Let me know if I'm wanted."

"Never sweat," said Randal, as he went down. "You can't be everywhere. There's many another day at the back of Mow Cop."

Thomas jerked. "Eh?"

John smiled at him. "No need to look out all the time," he said. "We'll likely hear them before we see them."

They watched the smoke above Crewe.

"You're not vexed?"

"At you?"

Thomas nodded.

"Why should I be?"

"I was wrong road round, wasn't I?"

"Were you? I thought it was pretty clever to be guarding the east side as well. You could save us from a sneak attack."

"That's right."

"One thing, though. You were a bit obvious. A good soldier uses cover better. Is your musket primed?"

"Yes, John."

"Then point it somewhere else, and not at me."

"Yes, John."

"Randal says you weren't talking."

"I wasn't. I was thinking. Lots."

"Ay?"

Thomas squatted below the wall. He was silent.

"Is anything the matter?" said John.

"No."

"Would you like to go to Margery?"

"I can do sentry same as the best!"

"Where's the thunderstone?"

"I give it her before I come up."

"You seem out of sorts."

"I'm all right."

"Why keep watching Mow Cop?"

"I don't! I don't!"

"Thomas! Put your musket down! Now! Thomas!"
The musket slid against the tower.

"I'm all right. I'm not badly."

John went to him.

"I'm not badly."

"What's to do, then?"

"Nothing."

"Tell me about nothing. I may be able to help."

"Happen."

"What is it?"

"I've wet me."

"Couldn't you—?"

"No. I was that scared, and sudden like, and frit—"

"We're all scared," said John.

"But I thought I was scared for Madge. But I
wasn't. I'm scared for me. And I think so much on
her. She's so good."

"You love her."

"I do."

"Then don't be scared. You've had luck today,
finding the thunderstone. Even if the Irish come, and
things go wrong, you'll be all right. You're nothing to
do with me."

"She'll not leave. I'll not leave you."

"You'll not be foolish. You'll get away safe.
You've no children."

"That's not my fault! I know what they're saying!
It's not true!"

"You'll have them when you're ready."

"We will!"

"You're both fit."

"I wish I was badly."

"Why?"

"Then I'd be out of it. I'd not know."

"Margery would. You'd be leaving her."

Thomas sucked his sleeve.

"What's it like when you're badly?"

"I can't remember. Sometimes."

"What do you see?"

"How did you know?"

"Guessed."

"It's not real, what I see, when I'm badly."

"What isn't?"

"And colours: all them blues and whites: and sounds."

"What?"

"Noises."

"Do you hear words?"

"Not proper. I can't say. It's just before, when I've got to lie down quick, or else. All sorts. Echoes backwards."

"What do they mean?"

"I don't know."

"Do you see anything?"

"Oh, yes."

"What?"

"Nothing real."

"But what?"

"I don't know. They don't have names, don't these. I make them up. I see a face."

"Whose?"

"I don't know."

"Is it God?"

"Eh?"

"Do you see God?"

"How should I know? I've never."

"Tell me about the face."

"It's scared. It scares me. He's caught. He sees he's caught. I know him, but I can't tell where. Happen it's through being badly. I think I've seen him that many times. But I know all about him. Is it me?"

"I don't understand you," said John.

"Is it me? Is it me? Is it me? Is it me?"

"Thomas!"

"Is it me?" He shouted at the hills, as if they threatened him. "Is it?"

"Why were you watching Mow Cop when I came up?"

"I wasn't."

"Are you more scared of Mow Cop than of the Irish? Is it Thomas Venables you see?"

"Shut your trap, John Fowler."

"Is it Venables?"

Thomas had lost all his colour.

"He joined the army, didn't he?" said John. "So how can he be up Mow Cop?"

Thomas flailed at him, but there was no control, like a child, and John held him off with one hand. The unaimed fists swung beneath his long arm. He waited for the fury to be spent.

She came from behind, from the stair, and hit John with the full force of her body, back-handed, across the face. Thomas dropped, and she knelt, holding him.

John looked at her, trying to smile.

"How interesting—"

But her eyes were open like a cat's.

"I hope I live to see your coffin walk," she said.

He dared not speak again, but turned from them down the stone spiral, into the dark of the tower.

"What shall we do today?" said Jan.

"Come and see," said Tom. He led her round the corner from the station. Two bicycles were propped against a street lamp.

"The world's our oyster," he said.

"How did you manage it?"

"Easy. Well, luck and a bit of cheek. I was taking back the watering can my father borrows from Mr. Hulse, and I saw Lay-by Lil's bike outside her caravan. She hardly ever uses it: so I asked. I've said I'll paint her fence for her in the spring."

"But how've you got it here?"

"Ridden one-handed."

"In this cold?"

"What's frostbite between friends?"

"All that way? For me?"

75

"For us," said Tom. "Barthomley?"

They set off. Jan cranked the rusted pedals. "I oiled what I could," said Tom. "It needs running in."

"You need running in. You're not safe loose!"

Tom was so much taller than his mother's bicycle that he rode bow-legged. "You mean the velocipede?" He began to slap the road with his feet, in long, scissored strides. "It's perfectly safe."

"You ass!"

"Observe the effect of one asspower!" He straightened his legs, slid, and swung the bicycle off the ground. "It's the dual braking system."

"It must've been agony, riding these to Crewe."

"Never noticed. How're you doing?"

"Anything's better than having to cross that railway again."

"Did you realise that Basford sidings are two hundred and fifty metres across? I've checked on the Ordnance Survey. I'd no idea."

"I had, by the time you'd finished!"

"Do you want my gloves?"

"No, mine are OK."

They progressed.

"I forgot," said Jan. "Happy New Year."

"And a Merry Christmas."

"Thanks for the card. Did you get mine?"

"No."

"I sent one."

"I thought you hadn't."

"Love, I'm sorry—"

"I wasn't bothered. I thought you were saving. It must've got lost in the post."

"I'm sorry."

"It's the thought that counts," said Tom.

The church was quiet and empty. It was warm, smelt of oak and stone. Any noises from outside were made distant.

"I told you it'd still be here," said Jan. "Nothing changes."

"People do."

"Or your attitude towards them."

76

"That's perceptive."

"You condescending prig!" Jan laughed.

"Agreed. I'm too happy to argue. So if you've any complaints, now's the opportunity."

"Do you mean that?"

"Yes. Why? Have you?"

"One."

"What is it?"

"I wish you wouldn't talk about us—I mean the real, private us."

"Who with?"

"Your parents."

"I don't."

"I get letters from your mother: and she mentions what we've said."

"How? She can't. I never talk about us."

"She knows about here. Barthomley."

"She can't."

"She does. When I made that crack about the Rector."

"What crack?"

"In my letter. When I said he'd made the same mistakes about us as your parents did. I said she was a victim of hormones and circumstance. Was it necessary to tell her, just to score? Was it worth it?"

"Listen. I'm going mad or something. I've had three letters. Three. In two months."

"I write every week," said Jan. "You've not had them?"

He shook his head.

"Your mother's been opening my letters? Keeping them?"

He nodded.

"Jesus Christ."

"I'm glad we're here," said Tom. "I need this place. Do I look normal?"

"Yes."

"I've gone berserk. Can you tell? It needs a church. Hold me."

Jan cradled him. "Let it go," she said. "Let it go into the stone."

Tom screamed, and tried to stop.

"Let it go."

He was still. The church settled round them.

"They gave me a special present," said Tom. "For Christmas. For scholarships. For being good. It's a cassette player, with cans. They've been saving up. They've been trying to understand."

"You mustn't despise them. They can't widen their vision to include yours."

"The trouble is they're not in a textbook."

"It's happening everywhere," said Jan. "Mum and Dad spend their lives picking up the pieces."

"Fine. Great. Lovely field experiment, this."

"Don't."

"You tell them from me, it's cold on the dissecting table."

"Tom—"

"I'm sorry."

"What are you going to do?"

"Wax somewhat Draconian, the way I'm feeling right now."

"They don't mean to harm."

"That's the trouble. Hey, you know what the loving slobs did? They bought me the player—and no cassettes."

"Oh, no!"

They both laughed and were appalled.

"So what happens?"

"I lie there, pretending. They're more comfortable than the cans I used for work."

"Hasn't your father realised?"

"Yes. About a week later. He was mortified: gave me the cash."

"What did you buy?"

"I didn't. I saved it for this."

"So you're plugged in to nothing?"

"At least I can play whatever I want."

"That's like arguing that a stopped clock's the most accurate because it's right twice a day."

"Lewis Carroll," said Tom. "Now there's an idea." He went to the table and came back with a church guide and a pencil. "This'll sort the old bitch out." He drew a square on the plain back of the guide, and filled it with the alphabet. "I'll teach you Lewis Carroll's code, and we'll use it for your letters. If she can crack this she'll deserve a medal. It's quite simple—"

"I want some fresh air," said Tom. "Let's try for Mow Cop."

"Have we time?"

"Yes."

"Are you all right now? It's not spoilt the church?"

"I'm fine. As long as you can handle that code. I want to get somewhere high. Out of the mire."

The road was steep, too steep to ride. The mountain was scattered with houses, but the village was at the top, gritstone cottages lodged among crags. The crags were grotesque. Cliffs, needles and slabs overhung the air, and in between were the houses, clamped to the rock. Dead quarries had sculpted the summit, and on the pinnacle stood a round tower and an arch, as if left from a great building, where no finished building could ever have been. The folly castle.

Tom and Jan parked their bicycles and climbed. The tilted slabs were polished by the wind.

"It's fantastic!" shouted Jan.

"Terrific!"

The wind scoured and cleansed. Inside the castle was hollow, with no stairs.

"Are you cold?" said Tom.

"No. I can feel it, but I'm not cold."

To the north and east the Pennines led away. West and south was the plain, and Wales beyond.

"This is us," said Tom. "This is honest. Down there, in that sludge, all the filth, all the problems. We're free of them."

"Are we?"

"No, but it's a good image."

"Barthomley and Crewe are down there, as well as the caravans."

"Down there, up here: it doesn't matter as long as

79

we know. Mow Cop just coincides with the difference."

"Difference?"

"Between us up here and them down there."

"Are you saying you're superior?"

"Different." Tom stood outside the castle, on the cliff edge. "This is for us." Jan's hair blew across his face.

"Be careful."

"Clean wind and the smell of your hair. I can't stand heights. Strange."

They ate their sandwiches in a roofless cottage that was a filter for the wind. No more than collapsed walls and a fragment of gable were left.

"Fabulous, marvellous place," said Tom. "And us. Living. Breathing in and out: stupendous."

"I wonder how many people have come home here," said Jan. "How many babies. How many fires have been lit. How much of everything."

"And before that," said Tom. They lay by the hearth. He reached up to the stone of the lintel. "Millstone grit. It was a delta from a river that wore away mountains above Norway, not two spins of the galaxy ago. And before that?"

"I can't," said Jan. "It loses me. I stay with people. I love you."

"Rudheath and the Rector had better start worrying soon," said Tom.

"I know."

He stroked her hair.

"But not yet," said Jan.

"I know."

"You don't mind."

"I hope I wouldn't be so crass."

"I love you," said Jan.

"Tom's a-cold."

"Are you?"

"I'm not cold. I said Tom's a-cold."

"Good."

"There's something in the chimney."

"Don't move," said Jan. "It's our house."

80

"That's all I grudge," said Tom. "Being skint doesn't matter—but if we could let rip, just one time. Just a few hours without worry about money."

"I'm happy now," said Jan. "This will do me."

"But one day," said Tom, "we shall."

"One day. You're right: there is something in the chimney. It's smooth."

Jan knelt on the fallen rubbish that blocked the hearth. "It's cemented in. I can't move it. Be careful."

"I'll take away the other stones round it," said Tom. The mortar was perished, and he lifted the blocks away from the chimney breast. "It's a cavity. Here she comes—"

"It's beautiful!"

Tom brushed the dirt with his sleeve. He held a stone axe head. It filled his palm. He rubbed with wet grass, and the axe shone grey-green, polished, flawless. It tapered to a thin edge at one end, and the other was a hammer shape, pierced for hafting.

"It's very beautiful," said Tom.

"Let me hold it." Jan took it as if it were a delicate bird. "This is it," she said. "This is it. My real and special thing. Can we keep it? From our house?"

"Why not? A momentum of our visit. I doubt if the owner's still interested," said Tom. "But I am. Why wall it in?"

"A Bunty," said Jan. "A real thing." She started to cry.

"What's the matter?"

"I love you. I'm so happy."

"Crying?"

"I couldn't have pets, with moving, and dolls weren't real, and Mummy wasn't in, and when they were they were always busy or too tired, and we never made friends with moving, and I was so lonely, so alone, till you. I'd nothing till you. Nothing stayed. But you did. You rode those bikes. You came. You've never let anybody down. And now. We found it in our real house. We'll take turns to look after it, then we'll never be apart: this in your hand."

"Orion," said Tom. He held her. "There's no end

to you. I thought I had you worked out. I hadn't begun."

"My face is a mess."

"Your face is the most important thing I've ever seen."

"I'm crying again."

"So am I."

The bicycles flew down Mow Cop. They passed Barthomley in darkness. Their lamps wove on the hills. Crewe was a glowing sky.

Tom handed the axe to Jan.

"Hello."

"Hello."


She was grinding rye by the hut doorway. Macey fed the grain to the upperstone as it whirled and rang upon the cockhead of the nether, and the flour swept white arms in a curve.

"What do you see?"

"No Macey," he said.

"Has he gone?"

"I reckon."

"Where?"

He shrugged. "Some place better for killing."

"Do you want him back?"

"I'm not much, else."

"But you see more."

"I don't want to. If he came back, he wouldn't let me see, wouldn't Macey. But he's somewhere killing now. He won't help me."

"What do you see?"

"Frightened. Scared."

"Is it close? Do you see close?"

"I don't know. He's scared, caught, yes, both."

"Who?"

"Him. They're both."

"Can you go to him?"

"Yes."

"Go to him."

"Yes."

"Are you with him?"

82

"Yes."

"Who is he?"

"I don't know."

"Look at him."

"He—they—too scared. It's blue silver! Always blue silver! I want Macey!"

"Hush. It's all right."

"But I can't help my mates. Seeing lies is daft."

"No lies," she said.

"Where the hell am I?"

"With me," she said. "Won't I do?"

"Oh, you'll do!" he said, and laughed. "Happen I shan't let Macey back—in case he's jealous!"

She stroked his head. The mill stopped.

Magoo came into the hut and kicked Macey. "Out." He pulled the girl across to the dark side of the hut.

"You mustn't. Logan said."

"Logan knows what he can do."

"And he'll do it," said Logan. He picked Magoo up and threw him out of the door onto the rock, stunning him. Face watched from the summit.

"Why don't you go and find yourself some heads," said Logan, "and cool off, before I have to kill you?"

Magoo squirmed for breath. "I'd—like to—get yours—"

"You can't afford the luxury."

"I—bloody know—that—"

"You also know the girl's not to be touched. She might abort. You keep off her."

"Macey was in there."

"Macey can't hurt her."

"What's it matter, anyroad?"

"She's carrying the new Ninth."

"The what?"

"We breed. We reissue."

"One kid—!"

"It's a start."

"If it's a girl—"

"Then we build up stock."

Logan climbed to take over duty from Face.

Magoo examined his bruises. "That bugger thinks

he'll live for ever." He chose a sword, hung it on his back and went to patrol the limits of the mountain.

"Watch him," said Face to Logan. "See how he walks. He's used to crags. Where did he enlist?"

"Some place on the Danube, I think," said Logan. "Or the northern frontier. I forget. Why?"

"He's too good. He adapted just like that. And these heads. He's keen. He wants them. And you've seen him do it, no messing. The real thing."

"So? All you Celts do it."

"But none like the Mothers. He isn't acting. He is one."

"How?"

"Deserted? Re-enlisted, to get back home?"

"You sure?"

"I reckon. I know these tribes. And you should've seen him when you broke that snake. He was for shouting."

"What do you figure?"

"We're OK as long as we're on Mow Cop," said Face, "and as long as the Cats aren't over-run too much. But if he gets word to his own, he'll sell us down the river—and you first."

"He was in action at York. They were Mothers."

"Uniform," said Face. "It does things. And it makes no odds. If Mothers stopped feuding long enough, your lot wouldn't hold them. He was probably taking care of some family business at York."

"He was a member of the Imperial Roman Army, engaged in putting down insurgents."

"I don't care what he was doing in Latin," said Face, "but as far as Magoo's concerned, the Ninth would be a bunch of heavies dim enough not to spot they were being used."

"That's treason!"

"Rome's the biggest fall-guy the tribes have ever met."

"That's treason. We'd be OK, though, with Mothers? He'd fight?"

"Not now. Not if it meant going Roman. He's got the flavour again. He's tribal."

Face went down to the huts. He sat outside. The millstones rang on each other, and he saw the girl and Macey working by the door. The wind over the rocks kept his voice from Logan.

"Is the goddess to speak?" said Face.

"She is."

"Is there forgiveness?"

"There is."

"Is there mercy?"

"Through forgiveness."

"Is there another way?"

"No other."

"Is it the goddess who speaks?"

"It is."

"What is the forgiveness?"

"Death."

"How will the death come?"

"The goddess decides."

"And the girl?"

"She pities."

Face rose, and entered his hut.

"I didn't catch any of that," said Macey.

"Never mind."

"But I do! What's up? What's up with him? I've never seen him look so badly. He's clever: speaks Cat, Mother, Latin—all sorts."

"He did," she said.

"He's skriking! Listen!"

"He has lost Rome," she said, "and is tribal, far from his tribe."

"First I want a record shop," said Jan.

"Why?"

"I keep thinking of you listening to no music."

"We agreed—"

She waved an envelope at him. "I had a record token for Christmas."

"Try and cash it."

"No."

"We could do things with the money."

"The difference isn't worth it. I want to give you something."

"I'm pretty desperate, myself," said Tom.

"I want to commemorate Us."

"How's that, then? The title's interesting."

" 'Cross Track'! As if I'd ever forget—!"

"Basford sidings," said Tom. "Barthomley. Mow Cop. Let's have it."

"But it's for you. You may not like it."

"With that title, it can be the crummiest music ever, and I'll play it all my life," said Tom.

Jan bought the cassette with her record token, and they went out of the shop.

"Straight to Mow?"

"OK."

"But I'm not riding the last bit!"

"The gradient's only one in three, you weakling."

It was the end of winter, shoddy with cold.

They walked the bicycles up the last pitch.

"I'm thirsty," said Jan.

"I saw a couple of wells before. The inscriptions were highly moral."

"I don't want to drink the writing."

They found the wells, arched recesses in stone. *The Parson's Well: Keep Thyself Pure* and *The Squire's Well: To Do Good Forget Not*.

"Some option," said Jan. "They're both dry."

"It's the thought that counts."

They lay in their house and sucked droplets from the reeds that grew in the room.

"Matches," said Tom. "And applied intelligence." He pulled out several newspapers that had been wrapped next to his shirt.

"I thought you were more crackly than usual," said Jan.

"It's strange today," said Tom. "Floating."

"Limbo."

"Not easy. Somehow."

He lit a fire. The place had been used before. Charred lumps and branches were scattered about the site, and some were protected from the wet.

"Don't burn rafters," said Jan.

"There's a few old spars—"

"It's our house."

"It's others', too: has been."

" 'Nod Pete.' "

"Who?"

"Nod Pete," said Jan. "Graffiti people have strange names."

"And do strange things," said Tom. "One of them was either ten feet tall, could fly, or brought a ladder."

"Where?"

"Right at the top of the gable, scratched in the stone."

" 'I came back Mary.' "

"Was it to Mary, or by Mary?" said Tom. "I find it unutterably sad."

"We're unutterably lucky.—What's the matter?"

Tom's face had stiffened. "I can't take that one. That one."

Jan looked at the broken plaster.

" 'Pip loves Brian'?"

"Underneath. Right underneath. A girl wrote it. You can tell. Flat letters."

" 'not really now not any more.' What's wrong?"

"Everything. No punctuation. What does it mean? Did she come back Mary? Specially? Was it a shock? What happened between?"

"Is it so shattering?"

"Pip loves Brian. You couldn't ask for anything simpler. Why can't it be simple? You'd think they had it made. And then—no punctuation."

"She'd be lonely."

"Or nothing. That's worse. 'not really now not any more.' Finish. End."

Jan scratched the plaster with a stone. It fell from the wall, and she ground the lumps to wet dust.

"Gone," she said.

"They haven't."

"Oh, for God's sake!" Jan threw a piece of wood at the fire.

87

"Nothing's certain," said Tom.

"Two things are. And one is that everywhere's been good or bad for somebody at some time, so there's no point in moping about Pip and bloody Brian, whoever they were."

"What's the other thing?"

"I love you, of course."

"Do you believe in confusion at first sight?"

"What is it? You're not fit to take a sheep down a lane today. Come here. Tell me."

"Tom's a-cold."

"That's soon put right."

"I'm frightened."

"There's nothing to be afraid of."

"That's what frightens me."

"You're playing with words."

"They still frighten me."

"What is it?"

"It's worse playing with people."

"Oh. Parents?"

"I found your letters."

"Where?"

"In her old handbag. Not the one she uses. The old one, with thongs round the edges. She keeps it in a drawer. My birth certificate; insurance; school reports; letters about me from teachers: all that. The catch doesn't work. She uses string."

"What did you do?"

"I read them. Thanks."

"Then what?"

"Left them."

"She doesn't know?"

"I can't compromise."

"You dear fool."

"I read your words. She wouldn't understand them. They weren't spoilt."

"Do you want Barthomley? Would it be safer?"

"No. Here. Let's walk."

They climbed the rocks beyond the castle. Tom shook his head in the wind.

"That's better. Clean. She'd always looked after me."

"Has she kept the new letters?"

"She steamed the first one open, but when she saw the code and how you'd used ink that'd run, she gave over. Nothing's been said."

"Poor you."

"Not at all." He stood with his legs astride. "Where am I?"

"Are you being melodramatic?"

"Just daft."

"You're on Mow Cop."

"Is that all?"

"If it was, you wouldn't ask. Go on."

"My right leg," said Tom, "at this moment, is in the township of Odd Rode, in the parish of Astbury, in the hundred of Northwich, and the county and diocese of Chester, in the province of York. My left leg is in the township of Stadmorslow, in the parish of Wolstanton, in the hundred of Pirehill, in the county of Stafford, in the diocese of Lichfield, in the province of Canterbury. You see my predicament."

"Tom—"

"But," he skewed towards the castle, "it's worse in there. There, the map says, the boundary is undefined."

"Tom, I love you."

"It's raining bell-ropes. Why don't we shelter?"

"It's your turn to keep the Bunty," said Jan.

"Why do you call it that?"

"It—seems right."

"Fine."

"Will you manage the bikes in the rain?"

"Easy. How about you?"

"I'll dry off before Euston."

"I'm sorry it went a bit wrong today."

"It didn't."

"I take great joy in you. Rain isn't good for poached eggs."

"It isn't the rain."

"Jan."

"You're too vulnerable. Haven't you ever—? Was there nobody else before—?"

"Not enough to be a threat. But now. I can't conceive of existence without you. You're too valuable."

"That's a lot. You're asking."

"A future without your eyes?"

"Take the Bunty."

He put the axe in the saddlebag.

"Thanks for 'Cross Track.' I'll play it as soon as I'm home."

"Tom?"

"What?"

"You can love without being disloyal."

The rain was all about them.

"Where's the salt coming from? High tide?"

"You're kissing a mermaid."

"That's usually fatal, isn't it?"

"Invariably."

"Invaluable."

"Invulnerable?"

"Us."

"Hello."

"Hello."


"There's many another day at the back of Mow Cop," said Randal Hassall.

Thomas swung. "Eh?"

John smiled at him. Randal had left them and gone down.

"You're not vexed at me?" said Thomas.

"No."

"I was wrong road. They'll not come from up there, will they?"

"But we need a lookout so we don't have a sneak attack. Is your musket primed?"

"Yes."

"Then don't point it at me."

"Sorry."

They counted the smoke about Crewe.

"Randal said you weren't talking."

"I was thinking. Lots."

90

"Would you like to go to Margery?"

"I can do sentry same as the best."

"Where's the thunderstone?"

"I give it her before I come up."

"You seem borsant."

"I'm all right."

"Why do you keep watching Mow Cop?"

"I don't! I don't! Don't! Don't! Don't!"

"Musket! Thomas."

The tower wheeled about Mow Cop. Thomas felt his cheek grate the stone.

"I'm not badly. I'm not."

"What's wrong, then?"

"Nothing."

"Tell me. I want to help."

"Happen."

"We're all scared."

"I think that much on her. She's good."

"You love her."

"I do."

"Then don't be scared. You've had luck today, finding the thunderstone. You'll be all right. You're noth- to me."

"I'll not leave you."

"You'll get clear, and no messing," said John. "It's not as if you're skriking brats."

"That's our business! I know what they say, them and their laughing. But we can!"

"Are you starting a fit?"

"I wish I was. If I was badly, I'd not know."

"What's it like? What do you see?"

"Colours. All blues and whites. I hear things. Noises. Sounds. Like. Same as. I know he's sorry."

"Who?"

"He's scared. He's caught. I know him, but I can't tell him, I've seen him that often. But I know him. All about him, I do. Would you reckon he's me?"

"I'm not interested."

"John! Is it? Is it me?"

"You fool."

"Is it me? Is it me? Is it me? Is it me?"

91

"Why were you gawping at Mow Cop when I came up? Were you looking for Thomas Venables?"

"Shut your trap!"

"Is it Venables? He went for a soldier, didn't he? So how can he be up Mow Cop? How did you take Madge from him? It must've hurt. How did you manage? What's the secret? How is she?"

Thomas flailed at him, but John held him off with one hand. The helpless fists swung beneath John's long arm. He could do nothing about the mockery, the cold, bantering face.

"She has you, doesn't she? Not like Venables. He wouldn't come running. She didn't fancy that. She wants something she can bend, and Mow grit's too stiff, isn't it? Go on, cry, you great soft mardy."

She came from behind, and hit John back-handed across the face. Thomas fell into her arms, and she held him.

John tried to smile.

"Interesting," he said.

"I hope I live to see your coffin walk," said Margery.

He turned away, to the dark of the tower.

"There," she said, "I'm here. I'm here."

"Madge," wept Thomas.

"He's gone."

"I love you so much."

"I know."

"Why's John like that? He's always looked after me—learned me—all my life— I can't plunder what he's at. What does he want?"

Notes and open textbooks coverd Tom's bed. He examined the stone axe with a magnifying glass. "Cross Track" was low on his headphones. He compared references again. There was no doubt. He took a clean sheet of paper, and wrote, "Dear Rector—"

His mother shook his arm.

"Enough's enough."

"What?" He swivelled the cans.

"You've done enough. Scarcely a bite all day."

"Wasn't hungry."

"It's morbid."

"I must finish."

"What about the jig-saw?"

"What about it?"

"If we don't start, we'll not be through before your father comes home."

"Let me check," said Tom. "I've got to be right. You set the table, and I'll be with you by the time you're ready."

"It's no fun for me, all alone in there," said his mother. "The table's cleared."

"You could do the straight edges."

"It's not the same by yourself. Anyway, I've a good one this week. Circular."

"Heck," said Tom.

He left his work and followed his mother into the lounge. The table was ready, the fire as hot as it could be, a box of chocolates opened, and a flagon of sweet cider. Two glasses.

Tom sat down and rubbed his eyes.

"Morbid. What's all the delving for?"

"It'd take as long to explain." He began to spread the mound of jig-saw pieces over the table, turning them the right way up. His mother's hands darted for the edges. "I think you'd like chess." She did not answer. Her concentration matched his.

"I'm sorry I forgot it was jig-saw tonight." Their competition was to put the last piece in. "Can I see the picture?"

"No." Already she had completed the circle and was building into a quadrant.

"There's a lot of blue sky."

"You're good at that."

"What the title?"

" 'Romantic Cheshire.' "

"How many pictures?"

"Three. Pour the cider."

"Dad'll be late. It's Mess Night."

"That's why I bought a big one. A treat." She chose the marzipan.

Tom separated the different skies, then the obvious textures and the significant lines. His mother snatched wherever she saw a pattern.

"You can be pretty certain of Chester," said Tom. "It's favourite. I keep finding bits of legionaries with the wrong armour. Then there's quite a lot of thatch, and black-and-white timbering. It's the bluey-green I can't— Wait on." He left the table.

"Where are you off?"

"There's Mow Cop, isn't there?"

"Yes; all right. You do that bit."

"I've got to work."

"But it's jig-saw!"

"I've got to. I'm going out."

"Where?"

"Not far." He sat down at the table.

"What's wrong, love?"

"Nothing."

He looked at his mother.

"I've a decision to make."

"Is it her?"

"Who?"

"It's a question, isn't it? But since the last exhibition, I daren't open my mouth."

"Why?"

"You're that highly strung—"

"Mother—"

"Going off like a bottle of pop, and no cause—"

"Mother—"

"Neither sense nor reason. Is it her at the end, or her in London?"

"Eh?"

"I've been that worried. Whatever's driving you?"

" 'Her at the end'? Lay-by Lil?"

"But I daren't speak. Not after last time. I'd have my head bitten off. Or worse."

"Lil Greenwood? You thought I'd been to old Lil?"

"You have. You've been seen. At her caravan. I daren't tell your father."

"Look at me," said Tom. "No, not at my ear. Look

94

at me. You didn't even begin to think that. You know
you didn't."

"Well."

"I borrow Lil's bike when I go to see Jan at
Crewe."

The look slipped back to the jig-saw.

"I wouldn't put it past you," said his mother, and
gave a mock shiver.

Tom stood up. "You're saying more about you than
me."

"What are you doing now?"

"Going out."

"Where?"

"For a walk. I shan't be long."

"I'm lonely."

"And no wonder."

He went between the lakes to the M6. Cars dazzled. He looked across the flat water. Birds safe on
quicksand roosted, marking his presence. He felt the
texture of the motorway fence. There was grit in the
angle of a post. The rain had not taken all of Jan
away. In the spun flicker of light he could trace the
hollow of her scooping hand under the bank. But she
was going. No thing matched her presence. The galaxy turned faster than thought, but did not move for
him. Nothing stayed.

"Only poached eggs."

On the way back he saw that his father had come
home: he was not ready for his father yet. The cinder
road through the caravan site and the birch trees took
him by the lane. He crossed to the houses where Jan
had lived. He felt in his anorak pocket. The key was
there. He went to "The Limes": no lights showed but
the doorbell. He pressed it. The same chimes. His
muscles clenched. Whoever they are, they might have
had the decency: whoever. He pressed again. The
same lurch.

"Conditioned reflex."

Nobody came. He slid the key through the letter-
box, but pulled back before he had let go. The road

was quiet. He fitted the key in the lock. It turned. The door was open.

Tom went in. The smells of the building hurt. They were smells he had forgotten. The varnish, the plaster, the wood surprised him. He was not ready. Whoever they were, they still used half a lemon to clean the sink. Only Jan's mother had done that.

"Association of ideas."

But the lemon stung. There had been no change. He reached in the dark to the light switch. "Jan and Tom." She had pricked their names in the wallpaper with a pin, but newer wallpaper covered it.

"No need for that."

He walked into the living room. New smells mixed with the old, changing them now that he could see furniture and carpets, pictures. Everything wrong in the right room. The stone fireplace had been painted white, but he found the now shining fossil, its ribbed shell clotted. "How are you?" he said. It was all the Welsh he knew.

The rooms in the caravan were stale with beer and tobacco. Tom's mother had done most of the jig-saw. His father was watching television, but through bright, flat eyes. Tom switched the television off and stood in front of it. His mother did not notice, but his father said, "What the bloody hell."

Tom looked, but could not see his father in those eyes.

"Mother."

She held a piece of jig-saw, did not break her concentration. "Yes, love."

"I need help. Both of you."

Her head snapped up. She was in her eyes. "I knew it!"

"If you had known, you'd have spoken earlier," said Tom.

"What are you standing there for?" said his father. "Are you Excused Boots, or something?"

"Will you listen? Please."

"Well?"

"Are people more important than things?"

"Eh? Why's he talking like a blocked drain?"

"He's morbid."

"Are people more important?"

"Than what?"

"Things."

"Brooded on his bed all day. A few bits of jig-saw, and I suppose that's duty done for the next couple of years."

"Point of honour," said his father.

"What is?" said Tom. He leant over him, eager, ignorant of the breath, the eyes. "What is?"

"Skinful the night before, first on parade in the morning. That's our mob."

"Mother!"

"It depends, doesn't it?" she said. "All according to what you believe."

"Where do babies come from, sergeant-major?"

His father tried to focus his eyes. "Eh?"

"Mother, where do they come from?"

She picked up another piece of the jig-saw. "Now you're being hysterical. You know very well."

"Then who told me? Not you. I remember asking when I was seven. You were putting your hat on. I asked, and you said, 'You'll find out in good time.' I knew I mustn't ask again. But who would you blame? You? Me? Jan?"

"She's not, is she?" said his father.

"No. That's just an example—"

"Who knows what she gets up to in London," said his mother. "You want to watch that one. She could catch you yet, spin you any yarn. So you watch out, my lad. You make sure she can't put your name against it."

"What are we talking about?" said Tom.

"—Her."

"Jan?" said his father.

"We are not. We are not talking, we are not listening, we never have, but please, please, please, just for tonight. Are people more important than things?"

"As your mother said, it's all according—"

"Blood's thicker than water—"

97

"Please!"

"Aw, it's late," said his father. "Get to bed with your mithering. You make a better door than a window."

"Why?"

"Because."

"Because what?"

"Enough of your lip."

"You are a sot."

"Don't speak to your father like that!"

Tom turned on his mother. "If I ever speak to you," he said, "God help us all."

He went from the lounge. The caravan swayed. He heard his father's belt creak as it was unbuckled.

"He's not too big—"

"Mind my puzzle—"

But no one came. No one shouted. He reached his bed.

The bed was freshly made. Clean sheets. The candlewick cover taut. By his lamp there was a blue cane basket from among his toys which were still kept in a corner. The basket was for two velvet dogs, boggle glass-eyed: a mother and a puppy together, their tongues hanging out. His notes were bunched at random with the books under the bed. The axe had gone.

He tore at the dogs, and ran, one in each hand, by the throat.

"I'm sorry," said his father. "It was the beer talking."

"What've you done?" Tom shouted.

"Done, love?"

"My notes!"

"I could see you were over-working. Never mind just now: you're tired."

"Pip and sodding Pongo, for Christ's sake!" He threw the dogs at her, and missed.

"They were your favourites—"

"The stone axe."

"The what?"

"The stone!"

98

"Is that what it was? I thought you'd finished. I put it out."

Tom jumped down the caravan steps to the dustbin. He lifted the lid. The axe lay undamaged among tea leaves and soup tins. He picked it from the wet, and cleaned it, wiped the grease with his hand.

His parents were looking at him in the doorway. He looked at them.

"I forgot Orion."

"Language," said his father gently.

"I know," said Tom. "I know."

His mother had finished "A Quiet Corner," a thatched inn, black oak, white plaster. He recognised it. He had seen it from the graveyard at Barthomley.

"I'm glad it wasn't the church."

"Would you like something?" said his father. "A drop of scotch?"

"No. Thanks. I'm sorry. I'll not behave like that again."

"I thought you'd be tired," said his mother. "I made your bed specially. I thought you'd've had enough of all those papers."

"Thanks. Thanks," said Tom. "Good-night."

He put on his cans, and turned "Cross Track" up as far as it would go. The third time through, he fell asleep, and woke to the last hiss of the batteries. He would have to buy new.

Margery heard Thomas cry out. His voice echoed in the stair. She left the cooking and ran to him. She was in darkness, and pulled herself up the steps, her feet slipping on the narrow tread. When she came out into the light on the tower she was dazzled. Mow Cop was sharp behind the battlement, and then she saw Thomas. He was swearing, sobbing, trying to hit John Fowler: but John's long arm held him away by the head. His young, parson's face was twisted. She saw scorn, and play. She hit the face with all the force of her body. The arm drew back. Thomas stumbled, and she held him safe.

99

John Fowler stared at her, trying to smile, not to lose.

"How very interesting."

His sneer went directly to her.

"I hope I live to see your coffin walk," she said.

John ran for the dark of the tower.

"There," said Margery. "Give over skriking. He's gone. I'm here."

Thomas clung to her, and wept. "Oh, Madge. Madge. Madge."

"He's gone."

"I love you. I love you so much."

"I know. What's he been saying?"

"He's not kind."

"He's not."

"Madge, he's always looked after me—"

"He's clever."

"—learned me. All my life—"

"Clever."

"I can't plunder what he's at. What's he want?"

"What he can't get."


Magoo sat at his post, liming the hair of the heads he had brought in at dawn. Logan went the rounds.

"Why more?"

"Tribal. They expect it of Mothers. And I go in my own time, off duty. I like it."

"They know we're not Mothers."

"Speak for yourself."

"It's not jannock for the Ninth. The risk."

"'Jannock'?" said Magoo. "That's right military-manual dialect, that is. Jannock! You'd not last an hour off this mountain."

"How do you know so much? What was your tribe?"

Magoo smiled. "Don't worry about me. It's that Cat-humper we're landed with who'll break first."

"Face?"

"Look at him. He's never away from the slag. She's got him scared. He knows so much he believes it."

"What about?"

"Happen you'd best ask him yourself."

She sat with Macey, grinding rye. He offered to feed the stone, but she pushed his hand aside, and used only the grain from the jar that was by her.

Face was restless. He patrolled, watching her more than the boundary, scratching himself, frowning.

"What's wrong?" said Logan.

"She sent me away," said Face.

"You're under orders."

"Not that. She won't have my company today. She's singing."

"She often does."

"Listen. The tone. It's religious."

"I can't hear her words."

"She's doing something: different."

"Is it a festival?"

"Any day could be. It's not one of the big ones."

"Come on, then."

"No." Face held Logan. "We mustn't go near."

"Look, Mack," said Logan under his breath. "Pull out. You're the Ninth, not a gook."

"She's doing something differently. Differently."

"Maintain watch."

"Yessir."

"Leave baking to the catering corps. And you were right about Magoo. He's all Mother. We've problems."

She sang. The stone belled her voice.

"—You looked at me, you saw my face:

"You asked no question of my being—"

She fed the stone at each pause. Macey listened, happy.

"—Nor the hard stone from the earth,

"The goddess would not be grinding,

"If the girl knew nothing of the mill—"

The words were from the Big Words, he recognised them, but their meaning had to be left with her.

"—And I will tell you, gentle boy,

"It is with me the High Kings sleep.

"Bonded am I. My hands grind cold.

"The mill I turn. Hard for Logan."

101

"Are your hands cold? I'll warm them," said Macey.

"You mustn't touch me," she said. "Get the baking hot." She mixed the flour with water into flat loaves and made the bread. "Take it to them before it cools. They'll want it warm, against the wind. They're still nesh."

"She was doing something different," said Face. "I can't put a name by it—"

"I hope that bread's hot, lad," said Logan.

"It is," said Macey. "I hurried special."

"Take Magoo his."

"Right."

"Eh—is she up to any tricks, do you think?"

"I've been with her all day."

"And night," said Face. "But he wouldn't know."

Macey went back to the fire after delivering the loaf to Magoo.

"Where's mine?"

"We're finishing yesterday's," she said.

He grinned. "You think I'm nesh, really. Don't you? I'm not."

"Then get them crusts down you," she said. Her eyes were exhausted.

Magoo filled his mouth and ate. Face and Logan broke the bread. Steam came from it. They drank beer.

"Bit tacky," said Logan. "Grain's going off. Still, we've not done bad, considering."

"It stinks." Face washed his down. "Oily."

Logan sniffed his hands. "It's the flour. More like —fish?"

Face moaned, and grabbed the beer jar. He drank until he retched. He dropped the jar. It shattered on the stones and he clawed grass and heather and tried to swallow them, but choked. "Be sick! Be sick!" Logan acted: nothing came up. He gulped at sand. "What?" he shouted "What's done?"

"I knew. Something. Different." Face took his hand out of his throat. "I couldn't see. It was different. The stone. She turned it the other way. Flour. She ground it. Sun-setting."

Tom waited until his parents were in bed and all movement of the caravan had stopped. He made himself listen to "Cross Track." He left a note, saying, "Gone early, back late." He hid his bicycle under a hedge, and went over the fields to climb into the M6 service area. At that time it was not hard to find a lonely driver, and the night converged, M6 to M1, and he crossed the forecourt of Euston station while London was still quiet and the first birds were restless.

Inside the great hall, cleaners echoed. The departure and arrival boards ticked, rattled. The tempo was idle, but increased with the light. The place was warm, and the seats were not hard. But he could not settle. He patrolled, excited, his mouth dry, hands and feet tingling. Railway police stood at the top of the escalators of the Underground.

He went into the booking area and found the window she would use. He had a good hiding place behind the pillar in front of the First Class window. People came from all directions, but they channelled themselves along the same routes to buy their tickets. He would not be seen.

She would come up the escalator, round the policemen, to the queue. At the moment she asked for a day-return he would put his hand on hers and say, "Going somewhere?" Meanwhile, the chatter of the boards increased, footsteps built a rhythm and he counted the tesserae on the column. Forty, by forty-two, by seventy-five high. She would be early, to make sure of a seat.

She came along the forecourt, by the war memorial. He did not recognise her easily. It was her walk that was the same, and her hair. But her coat, her shoes, her dress: they were not for Mow Cop. He hed never seen them, nor the overnight case.

The man with her carried his coat. They must have come by taxi. His suit fitted him. The handkerchief in the pocket matched the tie and the shirt. His briefcase was new, and he did not have the time to remove airline labels. His hair was good, his shoes bright and he walked with his arm through Jan's.

He walked with her, past the booking office, towards the First Class window, towards Tom. Tom managed to go slowly about the pillar and not be seen. They passed him. The man bought a ticket and gave it to Jan. She took it, she accepted it, and then he gave her money and folded her hands over it. She put the money away and went with the man towards the platform barrier.

Tom bought his own ticket, single to Crewe, and followed. Jan was in the window of a First Class coach. The man stood on the platform, looking up, his hand on her sleeve.

Tom worked his way along inside the train until he could see them. They talked: his hand was on her arm, untroubled: the whistle blew. The man kissed her cheek, and the train moved gently away. Tom watched him. Their faces passed, a slow crossing, close, separated only by glass. The man waved, his eyes fixed ahead of Tom, and he was smiling.

At Basford sidings, Tom went to be near the exit steps when the train reached the platform. He ran up the steps, and waited outside the barrier for Jan. She came to him in her usual anorak and jeans, the walk and the hair the same.

"Where's the bike?"

"I've not got it today," said Tom.

"Never mind."

"Yes."

"Somewhere fresh."

"Right."

"Or do you want the Secret Path to Basford?"

"I want nothing secret."

"Oh. That's the mood, is it?"

"There's no mood."

"Have they been at you again?"

"Not enough for me to notice."

"Let's try this road," said Jan. "It's quite the vilest,

even for Crewe." It was straight, enclosed, and where the houses showed, they were mean. "You'll be radiant, by comparison."

They talked. "It's odd," said Jan. "There's always been something like this at some time when we meet, hasn't there?"

"Something what?"

"Not this acute: but something. As if we have to absorb the shock of meeting."

"The surprise?"

"Even resentment, for a few minutes. Almost, 'Why aren't you the same as your letters?' I think I've worked it out. The longer I'm away from you, the more certain my love for you becomes. Because we don't have each other, we have memories, and these memories simplify themselves. We forget our flaws and create ideals of each other. Then, when we meet, the difference shows. Instead of purity, we're people, the flaws seem criticisms, but the good part reasserts itself, and we balance. But it takes a while."

"Have you finished?"

"Yes."

"I was waiting for the bibliography."

"You've proved my point," said Jan.

"Impeccably."

"You wouldn't be so brutal in half an hour from now, would you?"

"Ah."

"Don't you agree?"

"Of course."

"I'm not allowed to get off so lightly after one of your intellectual safaris! You might discuss what I've said."

"There's no point. You're right."

"I love you," said Jan.

"We've not defined 'love.'"

"Why are you so cold?"

"My bladder's full."

"O, you who have suffered worse than this, even to this shall God appoint an end."

*Aeneid,* Book One."

105

"I can quote, can't I? You don't have the monopoly."

"But is the quotation applicable?"

"Use your eyes," said Jan. "This park was given by the London and North Western Railway Company A.D. 1887 to commemorate the Jubilee of Her Most Gracious Majesty Queen Victoria and the fiftieth anniversary of the opening of the Grand Junction Railway. There's bound to be somewhere to pee."

They walked down a long avenue towards a memorial. Every seat had a plaque.

" 'To the memory of Arthur Holland and the happy hours we spent in this beautiful park,' " said Tom. "Honesty. Simple."

"I was only trying to think like you've told me," said Jan.

"Every seat. A wife. A friend. Golden Wedding, look, and a son killed in action: two for the price of one. Why not? It usually is."

"There's the lavatory," said Jan.

"Simple, honest graffiti people," said Tom when he came out.

"In there?"

"Here." He began to walk across the grass. "The trees, too. One for Edward the Seventh. One guaranteed from the Mount of Olives. They look after you here. The loving and the dead. Even that soldier on top of the war memorial has a lightning conductor up his jacksie."

"A beautiful park, at the end of a vile road?" said Jan. "You're seeing more, aren't you? You're not just being wet?"

"So many people have made the effort to commemorate, to mark the flux. We've not."

"We're still living it."

"We've not tried."

"You're maudlin," said Jan.

"I tried so hard."

"How does this square with your new social conscience?" said Jan. They were at a derelict bandstand, " 'The Verdun Plot,' " she read. " 'These trees were

106

grown from seeds brought from Verdun, France, 1918.' "

"Shit!"

"A few honest trees?"

"I'm thirsty."

"For nearly a million men?"

"I'm thirsty." He put his face against the wet bark. "One of the iron crosses in our caravan came from Verdun. These trees should bleed. Something should."

"Can I help?"

"I doubt it."

"I'm not that furniture salesman."

"No."

"Tell me."

His face was still against the tree. He banged his head gently with one fist and held Jan close to him.

"There's something very wrong inside here, I'm afraid."

"Tell me."

He left the tree. "That was pathetic," he said. "You were right: maudlin self-indulgence. Like my father on the beer."

"Tell me."

"You've not come all this way to be miserable. You said so."

"I know desperation when I see it."

"Do you?"

"We mustn't live unreal. It can't be sweetness and light every time."

"But we can try," said Tom. "Main gate in ten minutes." He ran along the avenue.

"Why?"

But he could not hear.

Tom was waiting when Jan arrived. "What are you doing?" she said.

"You'll find out."

A taxi stopped by them, and Tom opened the door. Jan looked.

"What?"

"In you get."

"But—"

"Shopping precinct," Tom said to the driver. He sat back in the comfort.

"I rang from a call box."

"Why?"

"Today, we commemorate."

"How?"

"You'll see."

At the precinct Tom gave the driver a pound note and walked away, linking his arm through Jan's. He went into the warm, smoke-filled room, stepped over the children and sat before two lighted panels. An attendant gave him change, and he divided it into two equal columns.

"Play," he said to Jan.

"I—I've never—"

"Then watch. You'll pick it up."

The coloured balls danced, the voice called and the numbers clicked in the panels. Jan sat, and did not move. Tom fed her machine with money and controlled her panel by using her hand as a twig to mark the numbers. She cried, making no noise, and the concentration of the room was untouched.

"They can't be dim," said Tom. "It takes a bit of effort to run both games simultaneously, and that's how most of them play—although sustained repetition would off-set the inferior intelligence. I must reassess my attitude towards plebeian culture."

Jan cried herself out.

"We'll lose one pound fifty an hour each, at this rate," said Tom.

They did. Tom thanked the attendant, and left.

Jan was white. She had to run to stay with him. "What was that for?" she said.

"I object to cosmic Bingo. The Crewe variety is less damaging."

"Have you gone crazy?"

"Not at all. My appetite is ready to do justice to the meal I've booked. It's a pity we're not more suitably dressed, but they'll let us in.'

he waiter held Jan's chair. The tablecloth was

108

stiff, clean linen. Tom ordered flawlessly and asked for the wine list.

"What the hell's going on?" said Jan.

" 'I don't know' is the answer to your question."

"Are you sick?"

"I don't know."

"If you won't give me a straight answer, I'll stand on this table and scream."

He looked directly at her. His calm eyes were steady and their violence hurt.

"Which would be a silly thing to do."

"I shall."

"I believe you," said Tom. "Some time ago I put up the hypothesis that it would be beneficial to let rip, to forget money, to commemorate us. The park showed it could be done. We're doing it. Right?"

"We don't need to commemorate," said Jan. "We've so much already. You've spent a train fare. We've spent a weekend."

"That's just what we haven't. A bottle of number seventeen, please," he said to the wine waiter. "Do you love me?"

"Yes," said Jan.

"Then think about it, and don't spoil today."

"I'll try."

"You look more shocked than amused."

"That's it," said Jan "Your eyes. Shock. Has anything happened at home?"

"Something's always happening at home: lots and lots of nothing." He tasted the wine. "Thank you," he said to the waiter. The waiter nodded, and filled Jan's glass.

"It's Moselle," she said.

"Excellent with veal."

"You know it makes me sick."

"It was the lobster, not the wine. Wasn't it?"

"Sorry. I've not got used: I'm trying to catch up: sorry."

"Used to what?"

"All bloody this! No." She reached out her hand and gripped his. "No. I'm sorry."

Tom raised his glass. "To Us, then."

"Yes. To the Us."

"And not the glorious dead Geman grape."

He watched her eat every course. They had coffee and he paid the bill.

A taxi was waiting when they left the hotel.

"Mow Cop, please," said Tom.

Jan said, "Is this what you want?"

"Yes."

"Right."

The gradient made the taxi use all its gears. Tom sat with his arm around Jan, her head on his shoulder. They went to the castle, and again Tom paid too much.

They stood by the folly, on the cliff edge. The wind blew Jan's hair across Tom's face. He chewed strands, and stared down at the drop.

"I've absolutely no head for heights," he said, "but your hair makes everything all right. What shampoo do you use? Look at the unfinished millstones cut in the rocks. Aren't they terrific? Order swelling out of chaos. I suffer from acrophobia rather than vertigo. It can be insidious. I'm glad they let us eat in these clothes, aren't you? You'd've been cold if you'd come in your green coat and dress. Up here, I mean. Too cold. Wouldn't you?"

"They were Christmas presents. I didn't tell you."

"Where's your overnight case?"

"I leave it at the bookstall. She doesn't charge. Why didn't you meet me properly, if you saw? Why the stupidity of pretending at the barrier? We could've been together longer."

"It's my way. Why do you travel in different clothes?"

"To give myself a lift—to get through the parting bit—to—to— I change on the train. You wouldn't see my coat. Only my case—"

It was as if someone were hitting her. The thoughts smashed in. Tom pulled her away from the cliff to the shelter of the castle.

"What I've always wondered," said Tom, "is

110

whether they give you an extra matching handkerchief for blowing your nose. Or is there just the one, to match the tie and the shirt?"

"What have you done?"

"A lot," said Tom. "But, for the moment, I have believed that there is a single person in all time and space who is honest, and that I have found her. I have believed that she accepted me, and that I could trust her. I have believed in perfection. I did not believe that perfection came slumming to Crewe on a First Class ticket that was paid for in advance. I have been to London to look at the Queen, or, rather, the foundation stone she laid at Euston station, near the booking office. I have hitch-hiked to save the precious money for a surprise. I have waited by the window. I have been with you for two hours longer than usual today, but I have travelled Second Class."

"Do you want the truth?" said Jan.

"Have you ever lied to me?"

"In this. And only by not saying."

"Can I take it?"

"I don't know."

"I've worked out most of the permutations. The truth may be better. If you tell it. But not here. Not the castle. The boundary's undefined."

"Our house?"

"You're calm."

"Come along." She led him across the rocks. He was listless, and yawned, even in the wind.

She put him in a corner of the ruin, near the fireplace. She stood for a long time where the door had been, and watched the clouds moving from Wales.

"I'll tell you," she said. "But what do you think, first? It won't alter what I say."

"I read his luggage. I heard him. I watched him. He knows what he's after, and is used to getting it. He's the wine grower you stayed with in Germany last Easter."

"Yes."

"You fell in love with him."

"Yes."

111

"He's nearly twice your age, rich, sure of himself," Tom's voice was a monotone, "and therefore has outgrown bike rides to Barthomley."

"Yes."

"You slept with him."

"Yes."

"Come here." Tom held her, held on to her. "Who made the running?"

"Both of us."

"God damn my mother."

"Why?"

"For being right."

"That's not fair."

"It's true."

"Not true."

"Tell me the rest, while I'm safe. Why you string me along. Why you bother to come here. Why me at all."

"I love you."

"You do throw that word around. You love him."

"No. It's because of him I know I love you."

"Never tell me his name."

"Right."

"And I thought two-fisted Bingo was exacting. No wonder you weren't interested. What's Bingo to an international Lay-by Lil?"

"Now listen!" Jan sat up, shouting. "You bloody listen!"

"Don't swear. I might just start, too."

"I wish you would. I'm scared stiff you're going to kill me."

"Guilt."

"Yes! All right! But listen!"

"I don't want to."

"Will you hear me?"

"I didn't say I wouldn't."

"I went," said Jan, "because of another mess. Every boy I'd known, I'd let down. I went to Germany to get away. You don't know what loneliness is. My parents. They understand. They understand all the time, but time's what they never have. Time's for others. They work so hard, they do so much, I've worshipped them.

I know I'm the price they pay, and I can't begin to criticise them. But loneliness—and girls at school, talking, boasting, wondering. I thought I was abnormal—"

"Obsessed."

"I was. I was lonely. You have you. You know you're better than the rest."

"I wasn't better than you."

"Don't stop me. I must say it only once."

"I wasn't better—"

"He was kind. He flattered me. He took notice."

"Of course."

"I knew what I was doing. But just for once to be treated as if—I knew, I knew. I'm going to give you the worst now."

"I don't want to—"

"Listen," said Jan. "Listen to this filth. It was not filth. He said come to his room for a book to read if I couldn't sleep. I went. In my pyjamas. Are you listening? There wasn't a book. He was kind, and warm and considerate, and he knew I was scared, and he didn't hurt me, and he promised nothing. We both knew. I was so grateful to that man—but nothing else. He didn't reach me. I went back every night, to that warm man. It was only warmth. He never reached me. But he let me become what you felt the day I got home. You said it was the first time you really saw me. That's why. He made us possible. What we have was never before. You reached me without touching. Because I'd changed. Don't blame him. He never reached me."

"Is he married?"

"Yes."

"Children?"

"Two."

"Naturally."

"His wife—"

"Doesn't understand him."

"—was pregnant. He loves her."

"Why?"

"Why what?"

113

"Why isn't it ever going to be like it could have been?"

"That's up to us."

"Him. He's—seen—touched—where—I haven't— krauts—father—you tinpan bitch—you kissed me less than a month after."

"Look!" Jan snatched his head round. "Look at my eyes! That's me! He never saw that! No one's seen that!"

Tom spat in her face. She wiped it, and picked up a lump of rock. The edge was sharp, and she dragged the gritstone harshness over the back of her hand slowly. Tom watched the moment of ragged white before the blood.

"It stops," she said. "By next week there'll be no mark. I'm not hurt. The me that matters isn't touched. I'm unchanged."

"I can't—" Tom held out his arms. "Jan—" She went to him and he held her. She carried the pain of his strength without a sound, and raised her head when she felt his tears. As he looked at her, he retched, and threw her from him, slamming her body against the wall, and caught her as she fell, held her as if he were a woman, such gentleness.

"I love you," he said.

She could not breathe. He was still crying. "I'm sorry: I'm sorry. My head knows. The rest will catch up. I'm sorry."

"I've wanted—"

"I'm sorry, I'm sorry."

"—to tell you."

"It doesn't matter."

"I never wrote to him, or anything. That's what to-day was. He was going through London. He was worried. I thought I hated him now. I don't. But I thought he could help us. Have one day like you wanted. He says he hopes we're always happy. He gave the money to both of us. He's gone."

"I made you drink that Moselle."

"I understand."

"I wish I didn't. How's your hand?"

114

"Bleeding."

"Ribs?"

"They'll mend."

"I'm sorry."

"I'm not. It was worth everything to let you say it."

"What?"

"You've said you love me."

"High tides and mermaids on Mow Cop would have serious implications for Cheshire."

"We'd better descend."

"That money he gave—we'll need it for a taxi. I'm skint."

"That's all right."

The journey back was quiet.

"I've made a fool of myself," said Tom. "Wasting that money."

"I'd made a bigger fool of me," said Jan. "But we're OK. Aren't we?"

"Yes."

"Don't come to the platform. We're saving. Just tell me again."

"I love you?"

"And give me the Bunty."

"It's not with me," said Tom.

"Sorry: it wouldn't be. I forgot."

"It was going to be such a day in London."

"I can't bear to leave you looking so ill."

"I'll be all right."

"Remember the Bunty."

"Yes."

"I love you!"

"Yes."

"Hello."

"Hello."


"Sit," said Face. "Hush now."

"What's up?" said Logan.

"We're dead."

"What?"

"It's quick always. No pain."

"Her?"

**115**

"Doesn't take long."

"Her?"

"Wait."

"Dead?"

"Mouth and hands tremble, then feel it."

"She killed my Ninth." Logan took his sword.

"Hush now." Face held him with no effort. "She carries your Ninth. If she dies, you'll not have lived."

"My mouth—"

"Hush now—"

"Ninth mounth—"

"Face and Logan: what're they doing?" said Macey. "Shall I go?"

"Leave them," she said.

"Hey, I'm thirsty!" It was Magoo shouting. "Let's have some beer!"

Macey picked up a jar.

"Watch him," she said. "If he attacks."

"Attacks?"

"Stand clear of him."

"Beer, lame-brain! Now!" Magoo was on the boundary. Macey ran down to him and gave him the jar. Magoo drank the full jar without stopping. "More."

"Not on duty. Logan said."

Magoo was rubbing his fingers, flexing them.

"Tell Logan it's his head next. Beer."

Macey caught the jar as it dropped from Magoo's hand. He retreated. Magoo turned towards the sky and the plain, and lifted his spear.

"My hands tremble!

"My mouth sings!

"I have been to the rock of the snake!

"Look! The snake is here! It fills the sky!

"The horned snake, guard of men!"

Macey scrambled back to the hut. She watched.

"Big Words! Big Words! Magoo has them!"

"No."

Magoo was striding the boundary, his weapons moved in the holy way of the Mothers. He shouted.

Macey slid down the rocks with more beer, but was frightened to approach.

"The snake of the dale, it cannot be reckoned!

"The snake of the fell, it will not die!

"Blue of the great heart, be with me!"

Macey called back, "They are Big Words! Listen!"

"The snake of the road, it will not be trodden!

"The snake of the fire, it will not lose its eye!

"The snake of the rain, the shining serpent!

"The Great One Snake, the Giver, the Taker!

"All here now! Now is their time!"

Macey ran between the hut and the boundary. Fear was on him. Magoo tossed his weapons, and caught them. Beyond him was open ground, and then the scrub, silent.

"I am the Son of the Furious Singer!

"Mother, be here and around and fill your sky!"

He jumped the boundary.

"No!" Macey screamed to him from shelter.

Like rain beginning, the spears came, skimming on the hard ground from all directions: and then the arrows. They sucked the air, and hit. Magoo brushed them off, but some had to find their way, there were so many. Magoo sang and roared. The arrows, the spears were dragging. They rustled as if they were a dry part of him. He stopped.

"Mother," he said, and only Macey heard him, "why have you emptied the sky?" He was dead.

Macey ran back. "He didn't stay on the mountain," she said.

"Cats!"

The scrub, the open ground were still.

"Big Words. I heard him."

"No."

"I need my Big Words. I need Macey. They're my mates."

A Cat war-cry echoed on the ridge. It was Face. He stood alone, armed. "He'll be safe," she said. "Go to him."

Face was moving in a different time. He knew Macey, but talked to other people, things. He spoke, but in all the words of Rome and the tribes. He seemed to be happy, and for Macey it was the only shield.

"I am well I hope you are can fight now you I. Why come not on Mow Cop yet all please but every not worry. I want know now all see same sky now soon."

Face did not stop. There was a line of torn shirt going red. The red shirt grew, and Face's words closed without end. When he fell, Macey saw the red dark on his back.

"Kid, watch your ass!" Logan whispered to him in Latin from a cleft rock. "We got most, but the rest is sneaking somewheres." His sword had ripped through Face.

"Logan?"

"We're deployed. Soon as they show, we hit: many as they like, with companies in reserve, and cavalry. I pulled in the Ninth, all the lovely bastards. When we go over that ridge, no fooling, when we go, there'll be the Ninth wide open behind us. You ready?"

"No!" Macey tried to reach her. "What can I do?" But she could not leave the hut. She could not walk.

"They think we're chicken." There was no enemy. "You ready? You flip for me, eh? Mintaka, baby? Here we go, then: wide open! Spaced out!" Logan stepped from protection onto the ledge.

"No," said Macey. "Logan. Sir. Mate. Logan. No." He was beyond him. Though he lay flat on the slab and stretched his hands he could not reach Logan.

"Spaced out!"

Logan managed to flap his arms twice before he hit rock. It was longer until his body stopped.

The sky, mountain, plain were empty. The wind blew grit. Macey got himself to the fire, and she held him to give him her strength. "It was the goddess," she said. "Those who sleep with her must die."

He spoke cleanly. "I couldn't help them. I couldn't flip. Now Macey's gone. No me. No Big Words. No use. They saw. I didn't. Even that I couldn't do for them. I'm wasted time. Even Magoo: even him: he saw. Take it. Take it from me."

"No," she said. "They saw nothing. You see real."

"Not now."

"Now."

"Not any more."

"More than ever. Someone must. Killing's finished. Macey'll be real soon."

Then he cried. "My mates. My brilliant mates." Only then.

"Now then, Madge. I'll look after him. Get where it's warm. You'll catch your death." Dick Steele put his hand on her shoulder.

"He's not fit," she said.

"He will be, unless you tell him contrary."

"He's not fit."

"Let him stand."

"I'm all right," said Thomas. "I can do sentry."

Margery went down the stair. "You look after him, think on."

"Have you heard anything?"

"No," said Thomas. "There's the smoke out by Basford."

"None nearer. Nobody crossing fields. They'll be in the lanes: so listen. If they don't burn dwellings we shan't see them till they're here."

"Yes, Dick."

"And I doubt they won't be on Mow Cop. Let's have you this side of the tower."

John went to the pulpit. "I'm taking my men out, father."

The Rector came down the steps to him. "You'd be better with us, John."

"No. We show them today. If they come, and see we're ready, I think they'll not try."

"You're as like to provoke them. They'll pull back and work something devilish to draw you out. Be with us here."

"We're too much of a risk for you."

"Even the Irish won't touch God at Christmas."

"The Barrow Hill's the only place we could fight from," said John. "I've not done it to spite you."

"That stockade's worse than useless," said the Rector. "It's a challenge you can't back up. You could've killed every Irish, one by one, from the hedges, but you can't beat hard men in the open. If you will play, make sure you always win."

"Why didn't you say that earlier?"

"I wasn't asked."

"They're better tactics than mine."

"Heart and head, John. They should know each other. Yours have never met."

"You make me angry."

"That stockade is pitiful: only the dead suffer by it."

"Why are you always right?" John was nearly crying.

"Not to diminish you."

"But you manage."

"Stay with us."

"Yes."

"That is your head."

"And where is your heart?" said John.

"In Basford and Crewe, killing the wolves around my lambs."

"Then why aren't you, for God's sake?"

"For God's sake."

"I hope so," said John, and left the pulpit.

"A dog that tastes blood must always be put down," said the Rector. "Mustn't he, John, or he'll turn on his own flock?"

"I'll best you, one of these days."

"But cunning, as well as clever. Heart and head."

The church was warm and beginning to stink.

John moved among the people, smiling, joking, talking quietly with certain men. The Rector took up his sermon as if he had only paused for breath. What he said was not heard, but his voice held the church together.

John met Margery at the bottom of the tower stair. They had to pass each other.

"I'm sorry," said Margery. "For what I said. It was Thomas. Don't bait him."

"Would I?"

"I don't know."

"And I'm sorry for what I said before we came to church."

"No need. It was true."

"My head, and your heart—"

"Best not, John."

"—meet in Thomas. Love him."

"I do."

"For himself, as much as for me."

He needed the dark in the tower. The rasp of stone against his hand gave him concentration. When he came onto the roof he was himself. Dick Steele and Thomas were together. Dick lifted a finger.

"We've heard them. A door's been smashed."

"That's why I said leave a few locked."

"We should've poisoned the water. We've always thought too late."

"We're staying in church."

"John?"

"It's my order."

"But this was where we showed them; both sides!"

"I remember. But we're not up to it. We haven't the means."

"So what's the game?"

"I don't know yet. I was too simple. There's a better way of stopping."

Dick Steele held a musket ball. "Lead stops a man," he said. "I'll not look further today."

"There'll always be more men. It's not men we've to stop."

"Now you're talking like him!"

"Chance would be a fine thing! He's down there, singing his psalms. Yet he's twice me. I've known I must best him for a long while: but I've just found what it is I must best. He's a killer."

"Who? Fanny Fowler—?"

John laughed. "It's all right. I'm not deaf. And I've

called him worse. Come on, we're needed in church. Some of the lads don't like the news."

"I bet they don't. When you've made up your mind you're going to cock your clogs—"

"—it's hard not to," said John.

"What must I do now?" said Thomas.

"Keep watch. Don't be seen. I'll send someone to be with you, and we'll organise the tower. But that musket's for leaning on, Thomas. You don't fire it."

"About when Madge came—"

"That's all right."

"I'm sorry."

"So am I."

"You didn't mean what I thought. I've been plundering it."

"Give over," said John. "There are more important things now."

"Are there? All right, John."

Alone on the church, Thomas looked at Mow Cop. The bare rocks were red with winter sun. They did not move, but when he turned, there seemed to be something. He yawned. He could see it only with the corner of his eye. He knew there was no castle on Mow Cop.

He heard metal clink. Thomas dropped below the parapet and scrambled round the tower three times before he could stop. He found his musket and used it to support himself. He looked out under the ear of a cat-headed gargoyle.

The Irish were in the lane at the foot of the Barrow Hill. Some were examining the stockade, dismantled, unfinished, and were laughing. Figures moved in all the gardens, and the noise of breaking furniture began. His own house door was open.

They had come along the lane like ferrets. Their strategy was not trained: it was natural. As men, they were ragged, without uniform, tired and starved, but they knew a discipline.

Clothing was important. Some from the houses was already being worn.

The main force watched the church. They would be

able to see the lights and hear the service. They appeared to be relaxed, or too exhausted to care. Thomas heard their voices: his leg trembled on the stone. They were local voices, not the sing-song of tinkers. He focussed his eyes. "John!" But his voice would not speak. He knew the men. They were from Barthomley and Crewe and all the districts around. They had been gone for years, but he knew them.

His own doorway was blocked. A man came out, but he seemed to be still looking for something, although he wore Thomas's other shirt, the warm one, his boots and his trousers. He stood in the garden, and Thomas tried to shout. Thomas Venables. Thomas Venables. He gibbered. Mow Cop encircled him, the ruin of its castle clear in the blue and white flashes of the winter sun.

He slumped in a corner, held his musket upright to stop the tower, but he could still see Thomas Venables in the blue and white light through the sandstone, and all the other things he saw. His fist clenched, and his finger jerked in spasm on the trigger.

John heard the shot and ran to the stair. Margery came, silent, but as quick. The black, spinning climb broke into the redness of the sun, and opposite the tower doorhead sat Thomas, helpless, his legs straight, the musket pointing to the sky, the powder haze of the shot still in the air.


Jan waited at the bottom of the Rectory drive. Tom was trying to get away from the Rector's enthusiasm in the porch.

"Thank you. Yes. Not at all—"

"Most gratifying—the curator—extraordinary—congratulated—significant advancement—"

"Thank you—"

Jan broke sticks.

"Any time, any time—keys through the letter-box—"

"What keys?" said Jan.

"To the church," said Tom. "I thought I'd better

123

stand by my original interest in his locked chapel and the monuments."

"Why did you have to go and see him?"

"He's quite a prominent academic."

"So?"

"I wrote to him. He was helpful."

"It sounded as though you'd been the helpful one."

"He's a lonely old man, and a specialist. That doesn't give him much chance to talk."

"Where do you come in?"

"Through the door," said Tom. "You asked for that!"

"Idiot. Two keys?"

"One's for the tower, but he says he can never remember which: and the view's good, if we want to go up."

"Why was I kept out of it?"

"He'd've felt obliged to give us coffee or something. I need to be with you."

"Can we sit in the church first, like we've always done?"

"Yes."

"It's been the worst gap."

"It has."

"What do you do with my letters?"

"Transpose into hieroglyph on the original, and burn the decode. We forgot to change the key words last time, by the way."

"I've never wanted to write so much. It chews me up. It's slow."

"There isn't a quicker code I'd dare risk against her."

"And I've lost Orion."

"I still see him."

"It's the buildings."

"He'll be back in the autumn. Shall we swap to a circumpolar star? They're aways there."

"I like Orion."

"How's London?"

"Fine. And Rudheath?"

"The usual struggle for destruction. Your parents?"

"I saw them on television last week."

"Great."

"Where are those monuments? What's so special they need to be behind bars?"

"Graffiti people, I expect. They're by the chancel." He unlocked the door.

In front of them lay a facsimile of a beautiful woman, carved in white marble.

" '1887.' I'd like to know why the Victorians were so loathsomely realistic. She doesn't look dead. It's more as if she's dropped in for a kip during the sermon. Pehaps they wanted better mementoes than a photograph."

"It gives me the creeps," said Jan. "The turn of her hand."

"Nurse! Where's your objectivity?"

"It went out of the window some weeks ago."

"These are better. They'd not hurt." One was a knight in armour, moustaches flowing over chain mail, his feet on a small lion. "Hello, puss." Tom stroked it. "Yes, it was graffiti that made them lock up. Would you want to hack him about so that your initials proved you were stupid?"

"It's only graffiti on bigger graffiti, all trying to say something."

"Still, who'd do that to the poor puss cat?" said Tom. "This one over here must've been the Rector. I could do with his skirt."

"Why?"

"There's red paint still in the folds."

"Why does that make it relevant?"

"Tell you later. Perhaps."

"I don't like this chapel," said Jan. "Go now?"

"What's wrong with it?"

"Perhaps it's that dead her."

"Perhaps."

"Perhaps perhaps perhaps perhaps—"

"It's life," said Tom. "There's a flux for you. Continental drift, five centimetres a year, and that—"

"Do buildings change, or is it us?"

"Both?"

Tom locked the chapel. Jan went to sit in a pew.

"It's to be expected," said Tom, "after last time. The pressures. I hardly dared come to Crewe. In case."

"I wish, I wish, I wish!"

"That's like 'perhaps.'"

"It's a good job I couldn't write it all. All the self-justification, the excuses. They caught up with me."

"We'd better change frequency," said Tom. "This church used to receive. Today it's transmitting. VHF Radio Barthomley."

"I want to get out."

"Me too."

In the graveyard the sun was shining.

"Better."

"What did you feel?" said Jan.

"Magnification. I think that place gives as good as it gets. Tom's a-cold."

"I was afraid you might never be again."

"You dear twit."

They stood in the shelter of the tower, holding each other, rocking with gentleness.

"I love you," said Jan.

"I'm coming to terms with it."

"—love you."

"But there's a gap."

"Where?"

"I know things, and feel things, but the wrong way round. That's me: all the right answers at none of the right times. I see and can't understand. I need to adjust my spectrum, pull myself away from the blue end. I could do with a red shift. Galaxies and Rectors have them. Why not me?"

Jan wanted no more than to hold him. His words vented. Meaning meant nothing. She wanted him to let the hurt go. He could talk for ever, but not stop holding her. Each second made him less dangerous. And she's not even listening. Why can't I use simple words? They don't stay simple long enough to be spoken. I have not come to terms with her eyes or the smell of her hair.

"I love you," said Jan.

"I think this key may well fit this lock," said Tom.

The tower door opened. It hung badly, and jarred on the floor. A tight stone spiral stair went up to the dark.

"You first," said Jan.

There were slits in the tower, but they made only fogs of light. The steps were narrow and the stone was without holds. Tom and Jan started up as if on rock, using their hands and feet on the steps.

They climbed to the ringers' room. A window led to the nave roof, and the bell-ropes hung in nooses. The church clock ticked, and filled the room with its clear sound: the escapement wheel jerked.

The room above was the belfry. It smelt of grease. The bells were upright, like iron flowers. Tom kept Jan back. "Stay out. They're set. If you touched them, they could kill you."

"Graffiti-people bells," said Jan. "Even they have to be inscribed: as if they didn't make enough racket."

*Peace and good neighborhood attend this parish.*

*We were all cast at Gloucester.*

*I to the church the living call,*
*And to the grave do summons all.*

"Metallic morons."

"Dad once tried to get the Noise Abatement Society to work on a Vicar," said Jan. "We were stuck between a church and a kennels. They shut the dogs up, but didn't want to know about the Vicar."

"What happened?"

"Dad borrowed a loudspeaker system, nailed it on our roof and linked to the hi-fi. We had Classics on Tuesdays and Pop on Thursdays."

"And?"

127

"He was prosecuted."

"He must have a great sense of humour."

"He needs it."

The steps were hollowed by use, slippery with twigs and pigeon droppings. There was no more light until they came to the top of the tower. They bent under the low doorhead and stood on the parapet.

"Quite some view," said Jan.

"There's Mow Cop."

They walked round, gradually losing the tension of height.

"The secret," said Tom, "is to look at something far away, and bring your eyes closer until you're used to it. Then the vertical isn't too bad. Oops."

Jan giggled. "Not the best demonstration." Her hair drifted in the light wind across Tom's face.

"I only have to smell your hair to feel as though I'm flying," said Tom. "I could flap my arms and go. That's acrophobia."

He climbed onto the platform of the doorhead. He was above the crenellations, and only the corner pinnacle of the tower held him.

"I'm not scared," he said, "which is why it's so dangerous."

Jan sat on the lead of the roof. It lifted gently from the parapet to the centre, a comfortable angle. "Did you bring the sandwiches?"

"They're in my anorak."

"I'm starving."

He jumped down to her.

"Was I supposed to react then?" she said.

"Yes."

"How?"

"I've no idea."

"You can make Spam: I'll say that for you."

They were out of the wind, in a clear sun. Jan lay back and relaxed. Their hands linked. Sounds were cut off below the parapet. They almost slept.

"It's here," said Jan. "It's come out of the church, up here: the peace: like squeezing toothpaste. Lead is a receptive metal."

"I'm hot."

"Take your shirt off."

She sat up and began to pull her sweater over her head.

"Don't!"

"It's all right, grandma: I thought it might be a sun-bathing day." His voice had been too urgent. She kicked at her jeans. "See?" She was wearing a bikini. "Remember when we went to the baths and had to cheat the bus fare?"

"Yes."

She lay back. The warmth of the lead drowned her. Silence. No movement. She held Tom's hand at peace.

After a long time she heard him say, "You're being either incredibly devious, irresponsible, callous or blind."

"What?" She felt sun-drugged.

"No wonder we had to keep talking. It's silence we can't carry any more."

"What?" She shaded her eyes. Tom had not moved. "I don't understand."

"I don't," he said.

"I love you."

"You say."

"You don't know?"

"I know I'm a lap behind."

"Dear God—"

"Someone else."

"You can't be a lap behind when there's no race."

"I'll not beg."

"It didn't matter," said Jan, "before. It didn't matter.

"That's right."

"You wanted to be with me—"

"That's right."

"—with me: not accessories."

"Yes."

"We were growing—"

"Yes."

"—towards everything."

129

"Yes."

"Then why spoil?"

"Fear."

"There's no need."

"True."

"Then don't try to make me perfect."

"It's more a question of priorities. I'll not beg."

"You'll not what?"

"I'll not beg."

"You'll not take."

"No. But I'll not beg."

"Who talks like that?"

"What?"

"That's not how you talk."

"What?"

"Who?"

"What?"

"Who begs?"

"Every Saturday."

"Tom?"

"I've worn cans—"

"Love?"

"—since I was eight."

She pressed her hands on her eyes.

"Saturdays and Mess Nights."

"Don't say it."

"But you've no idea how much a caravan moves."

"Is that it?"

"It comes to that."

"I didn't think."

"Oh, yes you did. Bikinis because it might be hot! You've a flavour for it. I know!"

"I love you."

"I wish you'd stop."

"Listen to me," said Jan. "Being together: OK? That's what I mean. That's what's new, important. The silences. OK? The bikini was a mistake: but only because I didn't understand. Don't cane ignorance. Please. I love you."

"Understand what?"

"Please. Tom."

130

"Understand that intelligence isn't the same as finesse? Understand that more of a caravan sticks to you than the smell of old fry-up. You're tearing me. You're tearing me. Bikini!"

"I'm trying to be honest! I didn't understand! It's my fault. I love you. I love you like nothing else."

"Bikini!"

"I love you."

"Bikini!"

"It's hurting you too much," said Jan. "I'll get rid of it."

"Have you caught up?" said Jan.

"Don't."

"I only want to know."

"I can't cry."

"Should you?"

"I was by myself."

"Yes."

"I'm sorry."

"You couldn't help it."

"Next time—"

It was Jan who cried. Tom held her, kissed her hair. "Next time," she said. "Is that all? Next time—"

"What can I do?" said Tom. "Make it better—"

"The Bunty. Let me hold the Bunty. That. And you hold me. You couldn't help it."

'Why is it a Bunty?"

"Please. I want the Bunty."

"I've not got it."

"I want Bunty."

"I can't."

"I don't know why Bunty. It's always been. Please."

"I've not got it."

"And hold me."

"I've not got it. I love you, and I haven't got it."

"Left it? Why?"

"I've not got it."

"Bunty."

"Not any more."

"Where?"·

"Do you know what it was?"

"A Bunty."

"What it really was."

They crouched together in the square of the roof, on the tower of the church.

"Hold me."

"It was an axe. Beaker Period. It was a votive axe. The best ever found."

" 'Was'?" said Jan. "Bunty 'was'?"

"It wasn't a Bunty. It was an artifact. Not a toy. It was three thousand five hundred years old, and it'd survived. Toting it about, we'd've dropped it sooner or later."

"What have you done?"

"It's where it should be."

"Where?"

"I told the Rector. He knew what to do. It's in the British Museum. You can go and see it. It has a label and everthing."

"We found it."

"Luckily. It could've been anyone. Kids."

"It's ours."

"It's not. The responsibility's too great."

"I wouldn't have dropped it."

"You don't know. And humping it around on the back of a bike. And the caravan. My mother chucked it into the dustbin once. It's not a toy."

"It's ours."

"It's not."

"Why?"

"—I sold it."

"You did what?"

"They paid. For that weekend."

"That was the money?"

"Yes."

"In a glass case?"

"You can see it any time."

"Touch?"

"Of course not."

"What's 'votive'?"

"Sacred, sort of."

132

"But you had to be told that," said Jan. "You didn't know: not without being told."

"I had to give it. It was too valuable."

" 'Give'? 'Valuable'?"

Jan went to the parapet, and leant over.

"Come back. People can see you."

"I knew. I thought you did. Shut away: no touching: a label. A number written on it: Indian ink: a catalogue."

"Come here," said Tom.

She moved slowly. "It's you," she said. "I've staked everything on you. But you know nothing. You tried to make me feel guilt. Dirt."

"It was for us. I did it for the best."

"Always for the best."

"Jan—"

"I love you," she said.

"Jan—"

"Do something."

He laid his cheek on the hot lead. He was crying and gulping breath. Her tears ran into her hair. She looked at the sun without flinching.

"A budgerigar," she said. "Mum and Dad were on a teaching course. I was six. I went to stay with friends up the road. I came in every day to feed him and clean his cage. But they told me he'd pined. That's a funny word. I buried him in a salad-cream jar. Poor Bunty. I had to leave him when we moved."

"I'll get it back. I'll buy it back."

"You don't know where we lived."

"I'll get it."

"Were you alone again that time?" she said. "I was. I'm cold."

"I'll get it back!"

"You can't."

"I didn't see how much it mattered."

"That's what you can't get back," said Jan.

"Next time—"

"It always will be next time."

Jan fastened her anorak. In the dark of the stair she could not feel which way the stone curved. Her hand gave the illusion, the stone reversing, inside, outside. The steps were dangerous hollows. She had to sit. Worn by so many feet, so long a time, they were not safe.

Tom put the keys through the Rectory letterbox.

"Never take me there again," she said.

"Right."

"And don't talk."

"Right."

They held each other at the barrier as they had held outside the tower.

"I love you," said Tom.

"Yes."

"Hello?"

"—Hello."


"What will you do with the axe?" she said.

"I don't know."

The bodies had been taken away in the night. No blood was on the mountain. Only a stake, wedged between rocks, was left. It carried Logan's head.

"He must wait while the ravens have finished," she said. "He killed here."

Macey kept looking at the ridge and the head, nursing the bundle at his shoulder.

"I should've saved them. It was my fault. All."

"The goddess drew them pictures, so they wouldn't be hurt. They don't know."

"Don't know they're dead."

"It's wrong to be under ravens. He was a good man."

"If I hadn't used it—to kill."

"You'd be dead. We'd not be here. A baby wouldn't be ready."

"I'm not fit. I used what's never used. Good or bad, I'm not fit. Macey's gone. I see bluesilver waking and sleeping, and red."

"That's real. Not pictures."

"Tell me."

"It's your god and your way. You must carry it."

"Will Cats come?"

"The goddess ground the flour, but my hand gave death on the mountain. I may not be free."

"I'll look after you."

"We've both betrayed. There'll be a price."

"I can't plunder it," he said. "Or you."

She held him closer. "Don't try."

"Face used to reckon," he said, "and he knew all sorts, that the more words people had for something, the more they thought on it. Well, if what he reckoned is true, I wish I was Greek."

"Why?"

"They'd words. Still have. For feeling."

"We've words, haven't we?"

"Face reckoned Greeks had more for this, what I feel. Romans don't."

"For instance?"

"Well, same as 'fond': but that's not enough. And 'wanting': that sounds too previous. It's no good: I haven't the words."

"You have," she said, "but you've not matched them till now. If they let me be, and don't part us, I'll find you words. And even now there's words they wouldn't kill."

"Why me? Lame-brain, goofball, screwed-up blue-silver—"

"Romans don't have the words. Forget them. They're ugly. I'll learn you. And think on: no matter what happens, it's a future, shared and held."

"Is it me?"

"Yes."

"Is it really me?"

"Yes."

"I know what to do, then."


"He's not badly, just frit."

"Look after him," said John. "I must go."

"He couldn't help it."

"I know."

Margery's calm fingers loosened the muscles of Thomas's jaw. His body jerked with breath. He tried to speak, but she would not let him.

"Hush, love."

Thomas relaxed into her. When he opened his eyes, she closed them. When he moved, she stilled him, as if from nightmare.

She heard sounds in the graveyard, and the echo of people on the stair, but all was unhurried, muted. Thomas slept a little. It was better when he slept.

The first warning was the thump of a musket butt against the church door. Thomas woke.

"John!"

"Hush. It's all right."

"It isn't. He doesn't know. I must tell him."

After the knock on the church door the echo in the tower became more rapid, uncontrolled. Her own body was hard. Thomas stood up and walked across the roof. A musket ball broke the crenellation near his head, and he went on hands and knees. The sound added to the tempo of the stair.

"Tell him what?"

"Not all Irish. Him. Mow Cop. He's there. I saw him."

"Thomas!"

She scrambled after him into the dark. They met people coming the other way, skirts and legs shuffling upwards in the stone tube.

Margery and Thomas were sworn at unknown, but they pushed their way down. Comforting words went along the chain. "John—" "John—" "John'll see us right—" "John knows what to do—" "John knows what he's at—" "John—" "John—" "John—" "John—" The bell-ringers' room was full, mainly the women with babies. Thomas went on down. He reached the church.

John was not easily seen. The Rector gave orders, marshalling the people to the stair, deploying the men about the church. John was only one of the men.

"John! He's here! Venables!"

It was as though the church ignited violence. There was no start to the fighting. The windows shattered and were black with headlong silhouettes. Swords and muskets filled all sound. A cow ran mad in the noise,

136

worse than a bull. It was the only saving against the Irish. It charged until it fell, and the Rector cut others free to run mad in turn, and he kicked the hens, anything to hold back the soldiers until the stair door was clear.

"Venables, John!"

But Margery was tugging him back, and the men pressed in, smelling of fear. The door slammed. "I've locked it," said John's voice. "Get up before they shoot!" They pulled to help each other at first, but there were too many stumbling. At the ringers' room they paused.

"Where's the Rector?"

"I'll look after you," said John.

Some of the women screamed, but neighbours slapped them quiet. John left two men to hold the stair below the room, and caught up with the line to the top of the tower. Fear had almost stopped them: there was movement without direction.

And then smoke. At first it was the sting of wood.

"They've stacked pews against the door!"

"Keep calm!" John shouted.

When the door burnt through, the stair sighed like a chimney. Heat swept up, air was sucked away.

"Don't panic!"

The soldiers laid wet and fouled rushes on the fire. There was less heat, but the smoke was like oil. Daylight showed amber above their heads, and they broke for the top of the tower. Some steps were cluttered, but no one cared, except not to fall themselves, and they spread clear of the smoke over the roof. The first to arrive had stood up and were dead. A steady volley covered the tower. The Irish were trained.

"Venables!" said Thomas.

"Yes, yes." John was crouching beside Dick Steele.

"He's sure," said Margery.

"There's one or two among that lot," said Dick Steele. "They're no more Irish than I am. They've been fighting there, that's all."

"Most part's the bottom end of every pig trough

137

from here to Chester," said Randal Hassall. "There's some as should've hanged these last twelve years."

"My father had to stay," said John. "To close the door. It drags."

"Ay."

"They're in the bushess," said Dick Steele, "and there's enough to keep our heads down, no messing."

"What'll they do?" said John. "They can't burn us out. They can't take the stair."

"They'll do something. They know what they're at."

"It's Thomas Venables, John. I saw him. I did. And he's wearing me breeches."

"Hush, now," said Margery. "John's busy."

"I've lost me musket."

"Never mind."

"Is he dead?"

"I've not seen him."

"Did you kill Mow Cop?" Thomas shouted. "Anybody?"

The people looked at him.

"I didn't see Thomas Venables," said Dick Steele, "but happen—"

"Come here, Dick," said John. "I must think."

"You'd best be doing, not thinking."

"Why muskets all the time?"

"To keep our heads down."

Screaming began again in the ringers' room.

"Ladders," said Randal. "Along the roof and through the window. They've got ringers' room."

The screams choked as the women tried to climb the stair.

"Help them!" said John.

But another scream stopped him. A man had jumped the parapet from outside: more followed, using swords.

Margery held Thomas. Only Thomas Venables would have had the daring to scale the tower: only he was dull enough to have no fear to try it. She watched him work, butcher and shepherd, driving the people to the stair. He had come in like a crow above her head. He went to the parapet and gave a signal. The shooting stopped. Then he saw Margery and Thomas in the corner.

"Hello, chuck," he said.

Thomas went for him bare-handed, but Thomas Venables tripped him headfirst down the stair. Margery ran without speaking, past the soldiers, into the smoke.

Two slow forces moved and met in the darkness. The women climbing with their babies, and the people driven down the tower. The steps were gone. Brief trampling smoothed them, and the first to lose balance on the soft incline brought the rest down. The stair was a line of bodies that stifled, all ways up.

Thomas Venables shouted to the soldiers on the ground. "You can put the fire out. They're thrutched."

The smoke cleared. Hands pulled from below, and feet pressed from above. The mass fell slowly down the tower, helpless in the dark where there were no holds.

The dead and suffocated were thrown out. The rest were kicked among the ashes to the door. Margery had not fainted. She saw the church and the bodies. The soldiers had begun looting the corpses of both sides. She felt for Thomas, hoping that he was near, hoping he had not lived, but he reached to her and held her. His strength was frightening. "Have you got it?" he said.

"Got?"

"Thunderstone: petticoat."

She felt its weight on her breast.

"Yes."

"I thought you might've dropped it, like." He smiled. "Eh, Madge, that was a do, wasn't it?"

The Rector stood outside the tower. With him was another man, an officer. They stood together.

The village men were lined up against the wall. John was next to Dick Steele.

"There's hope. It's an officer, not rabble."

"Rabble didn't plan that," said Dick.

"What do you reckon?"

"It's clog-cocking time."

"He's an officer. He respected my father's cloth."

"Bright-arsed rain," said Dick. "Look at his eyes. He's a flavour for it."

"My father's with him."

"You think he has any choice?"

The officer waited until Thomas Venables and the soldiers had cleared the towers. Then he spoke.

"Who fired on my men, against the King's Peace?"

"What's he mean?" said Thomas.

"Don't look at the Rector," Dick Steele said without moving his lips.

"That one has the face of a cur," said the officer. "I think it was that one." He stepped up to Randal Hassall and shot him in the head with a pistol.

"Don't move," said Dick Steele.

"We have one more piece of business," said the officer. "It does not involve the ladies. They may be excused." He spoke to the rector. "And my men, sir, have been most inhospitably treated."

"In God's Name!"

"In the King's. And I shall have any who give me more delay killed, sir."

Five of the twenty soldiers were left to guard the men, and they shouted encouragement and complaint: but each had their turn, and their anger was a part of the game.

"They are louts, sir. But they earn their keep, and one has to give them their heads now and again, or I fear they would prove intractable."

"I absolve them," said the Rector.

"You are kind, sir."

"And I curse you in the Name of the Father, and of the Son, and of the Holy Ghost."

"Amen."

There was not much commotion, and hardly any noise. Margery fell into wet grass, but the man above her was pulled away, and another face grinned: the face of a soldier, with streaks on his chin, grey from holding lead shot in his mouth.

"No."

"Now, Madge," said Thomas Venables. "Who else would you rather? It's been a long time, Madge."

She looked towards Thomas, helpless at the wall.

"No."

"Madge."

"Don't let him see my face."

"Keep the women here," said the officer. "Check for anybody in hiding."

"I love Thomas."

"I'll remember."

"Now the other matter, sir. You spoke of a father and a son." The Rector stared straight ahead. "Ah. I thought so."

The officer went forward. "I have a warrant for the arrest of John Fowler, clubman and mosstrooper against the King's Peace. Where is he?"

No one moved.

"Strip them."

But after the fighting and the stair, rank was hard to tell.

"Is this your son, sir?" The officer went to Jim Boughey.

"He is one of my children."

"Is he your son? Is he John Fowler?"

There was no answer.

"By heck, it's a thin wind," said Jim Boughey. "Or I'm nesh."

The officer nodded, and a soldier killed Jim Boughey with a sword.

"You could see his age!" shouted the Rector.

"You make the rules, sir. Which is John Fowler?"

No one moved or spoke.

The Rector took off his vestments.

"What are you doing?"

"It seems that only beasts are clothed today."

"As you wish, sir. Who is John Fowler? I see there is a choice of inns." He beckoned to a soldier. "Headquarters."

"Yessir."

"Drinking comes later. I'll have you shot if you anticipate."

"Yessir."

"Now then." The man next to Jim Boughey was killed. "Was that John Fowler?"

"No," said John.

"That is a cunning remark, don't you think, sir? It is a nice demonstration of my predicament."

"He'll kill the lot," said Thomas Venables. He still held Margery, as if claiming her. "One of them will."

"Who?"

"Our major or young Fowler. What's he at? He can't get away."

Another man died.

"Was that John Fowler?" said the officer. "Come, sir, you know him. Will you see all your lambs slaughtered?"

"My son's conscience is his own."

"Very well: let him put you all to bed with a shovel."

"What are you doing, John?" Margery shouted at the sky. "He won't stop."

"Follow your conscience and God's Will," said the Rector.

The major nodded. Women were beginning to cry again.

"John Fowler," said the major, "step forward."

The line of men moved from the wall together. Some were held up by their neighbours.

"I see," said the major, and nodded.

The Rector spoke from his blind face. "What does it prove, John? A martyr for Christ is his own man. Why make others answer for you?"

"We thought no end on him," shouted Margery. "He stood by us!"

"He stands with you now," said the major. "To your cost."

"I know who he is," said Margery.

"Shut your trap," said Thomas Venables.

"Keep your lady quiet, soldier."

"Yessir. Permission to speak, sir."

"Permission refused."

"He'll kill Thomas," said Margery.

142

"It's Fowler who'll kill him," said Thomas Venables.

Dick Steele walked forward. "I'm John Fowler."

"Thank you," said the major, and shot him. "Now who is John Fowler?"

Margery tried to scream, but Thomas Venables stifled the noise.

"You are an ordained minister," cried the Rector. "You serve: you do not command!"

The major waited.

"A most powerful, stiff and intemperate nature, sir."

"He's mad," said the Rector. "He was that way when he was a child. A feeder on the love of others."

"You hate him, sir."

"Hatred is love," said the Rector. He spoke out to the men. "You trusted in him to deliver you. He has not. You die for him and only him. John! Come forward. Now. In God's Name and your own."

There was no sign.

The Rector walked to the men and put his hand on John's shoulder. "This is my son. I baptized him John."

"Are you John Fowler?" said the major.

"I am and all." John spoke broad dialect. "Merry Christmas, Rector."

"Bastard!" said Thomas Venables. He pushed Margery aside and went to the line. "Out of my road," he said to the major. The major stood back. Thomas Venables took his sword three times through John Fowler.

"You waited until it was my turn, father," said John. "I'll be remembered."

"That was deliberate, soldier," said the major, "and skilled. You know where pain lies."

"He shoved me into nettles once. To see. Always someone else. Never him."

John's back was leaving trails on the stone as he fell. He looked at the Rector. "I bested you."

The soldiers had to use their muskets to keep the line.

" 'John Fowler, Bachelor of Arts, aged nineteen

years,' " the major read from his warrant. "A most promising young man, sir. The facial resemblance to yourself was outstanding. You may kill the others now," he said to the soldiers. "The sooner it's done, the sooner you may enjoy the village."

"Why?" said the Rector. "Nobody else."

"The major appeared to be surprised. "But there are those here who wouldn't betray your son. They may be dangerous, they may have knowledge. Yet I am a civilised man, sir. I don't enjoy torture. It's fruitless. Consider: if I torture these fellows, they will, eventually, say what I wish to hear: will it be true? If they volunteer without torture, they are cowards, and I would not trust them. If they don't speak, how can I know their thoughts? You see my dilemma. No, sir, it is a waste of time to deal with them. They are to be put down. It is the best way to proceed with their kind of people, for mercy to them is cruelty."

The killing began.

"I'll have no trouble from the women," the major ordered.

Thomas felt nothing real until he saw Thomas Venables in front of him with blood on his sword. He opened his mouth.

"Keep still," whispered Thomas Venables. "You've had your go at me today."

"I'll—"

"You'll stand. Don't move. But think on: if you don't look to her afterwards, I'll come from hell to give you what I gave Fowler."

Thomas watched the man. He was a brute made brutish. Nothing about him was clean but his weapons. They shone despite use. His hands and his eyes were armed. Whatever they did they would achieve. He had to trust them, to receive their skill.

"Right?"

"Be quick. I can't stop shivering."

"Good lad."

Thomas Venables pulled back and drove his sword through the ribs, a butcher's stroke, near to the heart.

In and out, once, and so to the next man, but with little care, and the next.

The Rector lifted his hand in blessing. "The Heavens declare the Glory of God; and the Firmament showeth His handy-work. One day telleth another, and one night certifieth another. Lord, now lettest Thou Thy servants depart in peace: according to Thy Word."

"He's not dead," said Thomas Venables to Margery. "He took it. Push off, mate," he said to a soldier, "this one's mine. Now, I can get you out of here with him, but after that you're on your own. Right?"

He picked Margery up and carried her across the Wulvarn to her house. When they were inside he shut the door.

"Listen. I'll fetch a pack mule. Night's no more than a mile away. That's all you've got. And he'll be dead if he's left longer, anyroad. Take what you need. No more."

"Thomas—"

He slammed the door.

Margery looked about her at the contents of her life. Then she moved. Blankets. Herbs. Bacon. The thunderstone in its petticoat.

Thomas Venables came back. "Don't take much. Where we're going, too much is dangerous. Come on, Madge: shape."

"I'm ready."

He lifted her pack.

"Is that all?"

"All that matters."

"Tom—"

"When I'm being—"

"Don't—"

"—most disgusting, I'm trying the hardest. Next time—"

"Please stop talking."

"All right."

"Please. The train's in."

145

"Yes. Hello."
"Hello."

Macey waited until her breathing was regular and deep. He made himself wait longer, holding the axe close to him in its tatters. Then he went out of the hut. The mountain turned beneath the skymill. He walked down to the boundary, and crossed it. Nothing happened. He heard nothing. From the scrub to the forest. Among the oaks the light was lost, but he kept his way by Orion and the White Road above.

After a while in the forest, he had to stop for the terror in him. But he fought it, seeing no blue and silver truths, only the branches. Yet there was escort: he felt it. He walked and did not run. His way was a procession for the tattered thing under his arm, and he would not break for fear, although fear was with him until the trees opened at the mound of Barthomley.

The burnt remained. There had been no occupation. He walked onto the long mound. His foot arched.

He already smelt of brandy. They found Thomas among the strewn white shapes at the tower. He was alive, and had not lost blood. They pulled clothes on him and lifted him up to the mule. He made a sound, but was unconscious.

"Will he do?" said Margery.

"He'll have to. Stick fast to him: don't let him fall. Watch his mouth: if it starts to run, tell me. And think on: I kill anybody as sees us, and any we meet, choose who it is."

"Where are we going?"

"Shut your gob."

He led the mule through the village. There was noise in every house. It had started.

They crossed the Sandbach road, keeping to the wood. He drank brandy from the bottle hanging from his shoulder. The sweat and fear and the light were behind them. They went into a safe dark.

As he drank, he sometimes spoke, but Margery

only listened. He was talking, and needed no answers.

"If he lives, see to him. He's taken it all today. He stood still. I'd not have. After that. I can't say as he'll live."

They forded a river. The stars were sharp, and the Milky Way spanned the valley. He looked up at the whiteness. "There's a few going home down Cow Lane tonight. There'll be more. I reckon it must be cold up there." And into the wood again.

"I'll dye, I'll dye my petticoat red,

"For the lad I love I'll bake my bread,

"And then my daddy would wish that I were dead;

"Sweet Willy in the morning among the rush!

"Shoorly, shoorly shoo gang rowl,

"Shoo gang lollymog, shoogergangalo,

"Sweet Willy in the moring among the rush! Eh, Madge? Remember?"

His walk was unsteady, but he knew the way.

"I've no words, save I'm on the beer. But listen, Madge. Where we're going. It's for while he mends. But I doubt it won't stay safe. If he mends, get him up Mow Cop. Go to me mother. She'll set you right. You'll have to fettle yourselves, but she'll speak for you. They're a close lot. Tell her I couldn't come. They're a close lot, and if there's trouble, you can see from there. Not down here. Go to me mother."

The ground was changing, opening to silver birch. It was damp, and a cold wind. Margery wrapped Thomas as well as she could.

"Where are we?"

"Shurrup." He was drinking hard.

"Where?"

"Rudheath."

"Oh, God—"

"But I doubt it won't last."

"It's a terrible place."

"You've been?"

"I've heard."

"It's favourite."

"How shall we fend?"

"I don't know as you will."

147

"Why here?"

"It was given us."

"Who?"

"Venables."

"But it's no one's."

"That's why Venables. Me grandfather, or some such, I don't know. Anyroad, he killed a dragon, they said, so they give him where it was at. Only because it's fit for nowt. That's Ventables."

He tethered the mule.

"Wait here."

He was gone less than an hour. When he came back he dropped a body from his shoulder. "He can go in the river later. Come on."

"Who—?"

"I don't know."

He led the mule deeper into the birch wood. All the ground was sour. They began to pass tents and shacks, booths, shelters of twigs and branches. It was a quiet place.

He stopped at a tent. A candle was alight inside, and there was a fire. Rags made a bed on the sand floor. Nothing else.

"Whose is it?"

"Yours. You've just met the feller as give it you."

He carried Thomas in and propped him against the tent pole.

"Here's a bottle of spirits I've kept. You'll need it. Save some against the wound turning badly. He'll as like be in a fever soon. But get him to me mother's as soon as he's fit. Don't stay here."

He left the tent.

She dabbed the hole in Thomas's chest with brandy and wrapped the petticoat round it. The thunderstone lay cool in her hand. She put it by the wound, and went outside.

The air was clean, and the booths were quiet in the starlight. There was no sound. Total stillness.

He was by the mule, drinking. She went to him.

"I want no thanks," he said. "I'll have no thanks."

"Tom."

"You stay with him. I've not changed, and you'd not change me."

"I know."

"I must get back to the lads. I'm missing out."

"Yes."

"And you think on."

"I feel safe here."

"Well, you're not."

"After today. The light. No noise."

"You get out. You hear me, Madge."

"It's sanctuary, they call it."

"So's a grave."

"What harm—"

"I'll show you what harm." He pulled her into the tent. He was drunk. He took his sword and thrashed the flat of the blade against his leg, and screamed like a woman. The candle swirled shadows, and the noise was harsh as Barthomley. Then he stopped. "Look now."

The booths were still peaceful, the light was still calm from the stars. No one moved. No one spoke. There was no sound.

"That's sanctuary. You're alone as you'll never be. It's Venables, Madge. They don't want to know. So you think on."

"I will."

"We'll not meet again, I reckon."

"No."

"So long, Madge."

"So long."


"Hello."

"Hello."

He rode the bicycles slowly. The neon of Crewe starred his eyes in the dark. The loss within him was too big. Each gain was loss now.

He reached Sandbach. Shop windows displayed the unattainable: smaller than stores, and worse because of that. He parked the bicycles outside an off-licence. He crossed the road to the bus station and car park, scuffing the ground, and picked up a lump of clinker.

He went back to the off-licence, the tears drying cold, and stood before the window. He calculated stress. The centre.

The window fell like guillotines. He reached over the sharpness and picked out a bottle of whisky, zipped it in his anorak without hurry, and rode away. Nobody seemed to mind.

At Rudheath the caravan tilted as he went in, swirling the trees.

"Had a good day?" said his father.

"Brought you a present. For both of you." He gave his parents the whisky.

"Eh up! How's that?"

"I play Bingo. You can't lose every time."

"Well, I'll go to Buxton—"

His mother took two glasses out of the cocktail cabinet. "Are you sure you won it?"

"No, I stole it."

"Don't be daft."

"Why can't it be a present? Take it, from me. Drink it."

"I can read you like a book." She poured herself a measure.

"I'd be better translated."

"You can be summonsed for riding two bikes," said his father. "It's a drop of good stuff."

"You're both intensely dear to me."

He went to his bed and put on the cans to play "Cross Track." The guitar moved backwards and forwards inside his head. The drums and bass were firm for the guitar to lead from, swooping chords, brilliant as eyes, but the man still could not do what he heard.

"Open the way. I'll take that road.

"I am the one of all gifts and all giving—"

"You bastard," she had said today.

"No such luck." He had tried to cover. "I'd always thought I must be the second recorded case of parthenogenesis."

"—Though sweet the morning, green the rush,

"When I get

"Cross track,

150

"I'll be

"Real soon."

The innocent words and the betrayed-music drove through.

"The stars are changed now.

"I did not bring them back.

"All systems went, but—"

"You need help. Mum and Dad say it's got to come from you."

"What, give it to an answering machine? 'Hello this is Tom Tom talking to Tam.' "

"It's their job."

"Our love?"

"There's a limit to debasement."

"De floor?"

"You would."

" 'Love is not love which alters when it alteration finds.' Remember?"

"—When I get

"Cross track,

"I'll be

"Real soon.

"Sweet is the morning, green is the rush,

"And all my loving is far away.

"The stars are changed, and

"When I get

"Cross track,

"I'll be

"Real soon."

Free of the words, the man tried to free the music. It was enormous. At the end the crowd would not listen, and their cheers almost drowned his exhausted apology to the bass, "I couldn't make it." But he had. He had.

"Give over sulking," said his mother.

He watched her.

"It's no use pretending." There was a coyness that drink gave her: and she was so old. "I can tell you're not listening to that thing. I'm not stupid, you know."

He looked where she looked. The lead from his cans had not been plugged in at the recorder.

\* \* \*

151

He went to the front of the mound, above the Wulvarn. That was always the sacred place. He had only his hands and a knife, but he dug. He dug as far as he could, his arm's distance into the ground. Then he took the axe. "It's all I can do. There's nowhere else. I'm not fit." He kissed the cool stone, and wrapped it tightly, and put the weight into the earth, and filled the hole, and covered it.

There was movement near him on the mound. She was watching. She sat on the mule, and had been watching him.

He lifted her down.

"Hold me," he said.

"That's why I'm here."

"Hold me. I'm not fit."

"You've no need," she said. "Not now."

"Bluesilver's close."

"I'm here."

She wiped his lips with brandy. He was conscious.

"It hurts, Madge."

"Sit against the pole. You'll be all right."

"What's this post? And the fence?"

"Don't worry: you'll be all right."

"John went to Chester. Saw the boats. He says there's waves when you're at the sea."

"Yes, love."

"He says they make a noise that comes and goes. Are we at the sea?"

"Yes, Thomas."

"I can hear them. And them lights all the time."

"Yes." She looked at the dark tent, the one candle.

"By heck, they don't half shift. Yellow when they're coming, and red when they're going. John never told me waves had lights. By heck, they're knocking on. It hurts, Madge."

"Have a drink."

"He's a close one, not saying about the lights."

"Ay."

"Why are we sitting out here against this fence?"

"I don't know, love."

\* \* \*

"You told your parents about me. It's worse than reading letters."

He stood in the arch of the castle, watching all Cheshire.

"I had to. I can't manage."

"So I'm just a patient. A number in a file."

"It's their job."

"You told them what had happened. You told about us. You told them— About us. You told—"

"They understood."

"No doubt there's a textbook reference that cures all."

"Each case is different."

"So I am a case."

"I have to see you that way, or I couldn't go on."

"You swapped opinions."

"It was on the phone."

"You must have minds like cess-pits."

"Like what? Now you listen! Who was upset because his parents couldn't talk about it when it wasn't true? Now it is, and my parents can, without blaming. Don't make us the cess-pit, love. Don't double-cross yourself. I'm the one who has to take it, and I don't know what to do. You used to give so much, oh, it was marvellous to be with, everything new and giving, like colour for the first time. Now you're all one thing, and I don't know what to do. Wherever we go I can't go again. No talk, no fun, just grab. Why?"

"Catch up," he said. "Rub out. My mistakes. My clumsiness. Next time it'll be all right, every time, and it isn't. Next time will make up for him—and me. Never. Poached eggs. Galactic. Red shift. The further they go, the faster they leave. The sky's emptying. God, this wind's cold."

He pulled her into the castle. The wind was scarcely less, making waves on the mud and water that covered the floor. He pressed her against the wall.

"Not here. Not like this. Not here. I can't take it."

"Neither can I," he said. "Neither can I, neither can I, neither can I, neither can I—"

"Tom! It's me!"

"It's Saturday night. Don't let words fool you. You're only young once."

She was crying. "No church—no house—no Bunty—"

"Shurrup."

"No you?"

"I'm cold. I'm cold."

She put her hands over her face.

"The boundary's undefined," he said.

"I want to be sick. I want."

"And so no more of Tom."

"I'd rather you'd hit me."

"It's cold."

"Cold enough to feel the warmth of your hand," she said.

"Your hands smell of thyme. I love you."

"You haven't the feeling. All words."

"I do love you."

"You sold the Bunty. You sold what I'd lacked. And you knew."

"Keep things in proportion, nurse. The bedpan's half empty, not half full. The axe was only a chunk of diorite."

"And what's that?"

"A dense, sedimentary—"

"Shut up!" She stood back, and spoke in a very calm voice. "It would like to go now, please. It feels sick. It's had enough. It has a train to catch."

"The only tune that he could play was over the hills and far away." He began to climb the inside of the castle, the folly, the empty stone.

"Tom?"

He climbed.

"Don't be so bloody dramatic!"

At the top he stood upright, jerkily, balancing against the air above the wall and the cliff.

"You'll not frighten me!"

He spread his arms and lifted his head to the sky. "Through the sharp hawthorn blow the winds," he shouted. "Who gives anything to poor Tom? Tom's a-cold! Bless thee from whirlwinds, starblasting, and taking!"

"Stop it! You're all quote! Every bit! And you call me second-hand!"

"Pillicock sat on Pillicock-hill. Halloo, halloo, loo, loo!"

"You can't put two words of your own together! Always someone else's feeling! Other people have to go to hell to find words for you! You're fire-proof!"

"Take heed o' the foul fiend. Obey thy parents; keep thy word justly; swear not; commit not with man's sworn spouse; set not thy sweet heart on proud array. Tom's a-cold."

"Tom!"

"Poor Tom's a-cold."

"Please, Tom—"

"Tom's a-cold!"

"Please—"

He took out of his anorak pocket all the family medals and the two German iron crosses and pinned them on his chest.

"Please."

"No words, no words: hush. Child Rowland to the dark tower came. His word was still."

"Axe gone. Macey gone. I can't see bluesilvers by myself."

"I'm here," she said.

"I was wrong."

"You're true now."

"Am I?"

"Silence forgives."

"Us?"

"Look."

The forest glinted with weapons turning away. Quietly they were alone. He held her.

"I'll watch," he said. "Bluesilvers. It might matter."

"Happen it does."

"You reckon?" He felt the child move.

"And I'm here."

"I've found words," he said. "For what I wanted to tell you. Oh, I know—I know—all sorts!"

"Why did you bring the medals?"

"The knights are drawing in."

"Why wear them?"

"For both sides. Him and me."

"Hadn't you better take them off? They'll upset people."

"You don't understand." At the barrier he showed a platform ticket. "Bought this morning. It seemed best."

"They're bonny lights."

"Aren't they?" She gave him brandy.

"I'm cold." His brow was sweat.

"You'll be better."

"You reckon?"

"And when you are, we'll go to Mow Cop—"

"I remember today—"

"—and we'll build us own house."

"—at the church, and that—"

"It'll be a good house." She wiped the blood that was coming in his mouth.

"It wasn't nice," he said.

"And when it's built, you'll put the thunderstone in the chimney, for luck."

"I didn't smash it. It feels that grand." His fingers moved over the cool stone, his face unseeing. "I mind a lot what he did at you."

"Try to forget."

"It's all right. I mean, same as, if you are."

"Don't."

"If you are: I'll be proud."

The red door closed. The blue and silver train. She stood at the window.

"See you."

"See you."

It doesn't matter. Not really now not any more.